The Convicts

ALSO BY IAIN LAWRENCE

B for Buster

The Lightkeeper's Daughter

Lord of the Nutcracker Men

Ghost Boy

THE HIGH SEAS TRILOGY
The Wreckers
The Smugglers
The Buccaneers

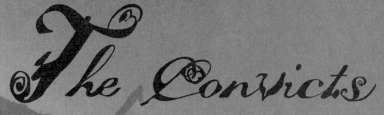

The Convicts

IAIN LAWRENCE

Delacorte Press

Published by
Delacorte Press
an imprint of
Random House Children's Books
a division of Random House, Inc.
New York

Visit us on the Web! www.randomhouse.com/kids
Educators and librarians, for a variety of teaching tools,
visit us at www.randomhouse.com/teachers

Library of Congress Cataloging-in-Publication Data

Lawrence, Iain.
The convicts / Iain Lawrence.
p.   cm.
Summary: His efforts to avenge his father's unjust imprisonment force
thirteen-year-old Tom Tin into the streets of nineteenth-century London, but
after he is convicted of murder, Tom is eventually sent to Australia where
he has a surprise reunion.
ISBN 0-385-73087-X (trade)—ISBN 0-385-90109-7 (glb)
[1. Prisoners—Fiction. 2. Runaways—Fiction. 3. Resourcefulness—Fiction.
4. Ocean travel—Fiction. 5. London (England)—History—19th century—
Fiction.] I. Title.
PZ7. L43545Co 2005
[Fic]—dc22
2004014968

Book design by Kenny Holcomb

Printed in the United States of America

April 2005

10 9 8 7 6 5 4 3 2 1

BVG

for Donald,

my little brother, but a big inspiration

contents

one
I BEGIN MY ADVENTURE

When she was six and I was eight, my little sister, Kitty, died. She fell from a bridge, into the Thames, and drowned before anyone could reach her. My mother was there when it happened. She heard a scream and turned to see my sister spinning through the air. She watched Kitty vanish into the eddies of brown water, and in that instant my mother's mind unhinged.

She put on mourning clothes of the blackest black and hid herself from head to toe, like a beetle in a shell. As the sun went up, as the sun went down, she stood over Kitty's grave. Her veils aflutter in the wind, her shawls drooping in the rain, she became a phantom of the churchyard, a figure feared by children. Even I, who had known her all my life, never ventured near the place when the yellow fogs of autumn came swirling round the headstones.

It was a day such as that, an autumn day, when my father had to drag her from my sister's grave. The fog was thick and putrid, like a vile custard poured among the tombstones. From the iron gate at the street I couldn't see as far as the church. But I saw the crosses and the marble angels, some distinct, some like shadows, and my father among them, as though battling with a demon. I heard my mother wailing.

Her boots were black, her bonnets black, and the rippling of her clothes made her look more like a beast than a person. She shrieked and fought against him, clinging to the headstone, clawing at the earth. When at last my father brought her through the gate, she was howling like a dog. In her hand was a fistful of dirt. She looked at it, and fainted dead away.

We lifted her into the cart, among the bundles and the chests that represented all our goods. The drayman climbed to his seat. He cracked his whip and swore at his horse, and off we started for Camden Town.

I walked beside my father as we passed our empty house and turned toward the bridge. By chance, the drayman chose the same route that Father took every morning on his useless treks to the Admiralty. I saw him look up at the house, then down at the ground, and we went along in silence. Only a few feet before me, the cart was no more than a gray shape. It seemed to be pulled by an invisible horse that snorted and wheezed as it clopped on the paving stones. My mother woke and sat keening on the cart.

We were nearly at the river before my father spoke. "This is for her own good," he said. "You know that, Tom."

"Yes," I said, though it wasn't true. We were not leaving Surrey for my mother's sake, but only to save the two pennies my father spent crossing the bridge every day. We were leaving because Mr. Goodfellow had driven us away, just as he had driven us from a larger house not a year before. I be-

2

lieved he would haunt us forever, chasing us from one shrinking home to the next, until he saw us out on the streets with the beggars and the blind. We were leaving Surrey because my father was a sailor without a ship.

He didn't walk like a sailor anymore. He didn't look like one, nor even smell like one, and I wouldn't have believed he had *ever* been a sailor if it weren't for the threadbare uniform he donned every morning, and for the bits of sailorly knickknack that had once filled our house but now were nearly gone. In all my life I had watched him sailing out to sea only once, and then in a thing so woeful that it sank before he reached the Medway. That, too, had been Mr. Goodfellow's doing; that had been the start of it.

When we reached the timber wharfs at the foot of the bridge I could feel the Thames close at hand. Foghorns hooted and moaned, and there came the thumping of a steamboat as it thrashed its way along the river. But I couldn't smell the water; the stench of the fog hid even that.

We paid our toll and started over the bridge. Father walked at the very edge, his sleeve smearing the soot that had fallen on the rail. Horses and carriages appeared before us, and a cabriolet came rattling up from behind. I had to dodge around people, and step nimbly from a curricle's path, but my father walked straight ahead with a mind only for the river below us. Ladies on the benches drew in their feet as he passed. One snatched up a little white dog. A man shouted, "Watch where you're walking." But Father just brushed by them all.

I imagined that he could somehow see the water, and all the life upon it. Sounds that drifted up to me as mere groans and puzzling splashes must, to him, have been visions of boatsmen and bargemen, of oars and sails at work. His head rose; his shoulders straightened for a moment.

3

I had no wish to know his world, though I had been born by the banks of the Thames, where the river met the sea. We'd left the village before I was two, at the wishes of my mother. The river had taken her father, and the sea had taken her brothers, and ever since my sister's death she'd taught me to fear them both. I often thought—when I saw the Thames swirling by—that one or the other was waiting to take me too.

It was a disappointment for my father that I had no interest in the ways of sailors. To see him now as a gray shape in the fog made me think how far apart we'd drifted. He believed that I had been badly coddled ever since my sister's death, and there may have been some truth in that. He wasn't proud of me, nor I of him.

Behind the drayman's creaking cart we walked for miles. We crossed the Strand, and Covent Garden with its crowded stalls, and threaded through a maze of narrow streets. As we started up Tottenham Court the fog began to fade around us, until we came out into sunshine with still a mile to go. Behind us it lay over the city like a yellow grout, and only the high dome of St. Paul's and its glittering cross stood in the brightness and blue.

The day was nearly spent when we arrived at our new home, a wretched little place squeezed into a row of others. Miles away, in the heart of London, a chorus of bells rang the hour. The drayman tossed our things from his cart and hurried away, as though he dreaded the thought of the coming night's finding him so far from the city. My mother climbed down by herself and stood in silence by the street, herself a figure of the night. There wasn't a soul in sight, and no one came to greet us.

I picked up a chest and carried it to the house, giving

Mother a dirty look as I passed, for she did nothing to help. When I stepped through the door, a herd of cockroaches stampeded down the hall. I stood for a moment in disgusted surprise, then thundered after them with stomping boots. But Father, coming behind me, shouted, "Stop that, Tom. Those are God's creatures."

"They're roaches," I said.

"God's roaches, then." He was carrying a chair that was almost too big to fit through the door. All I could see of him was his face above it and his feet below. "How would you like it, Tom, if some great creature tried to squash *you*?" he said. "They're only trying to get away. They're trying to hide. Wouldn't you do the same thing?"

"They're *cockroaches*," I said.

"Doesn't matter." He took the chair into the tiny parlor, craning his neck to see the floor where he walked. "Find the lamps and get them lit. Light alone will drive them off."

I watched the black things scurry away, pleased at least that they weren't rats. They filed into the dark dankness of our scullery, and my skin prickled at the sight and sound of the beetles. I knew that every night they would go roaming through the rooms, that I would find them thick as carpets when I rose before the sun.

"I hate him," I said.

"Who?"

"Mr. Goodfellow."

Father set his chair down. "Oh, we're not beaten yet, Tom," he said. "Not by a long shot."

"Well, it isn't fair," I said.

"Even a foul wind is fair if you come about."

His sailorly talk always befuddled me. I didn't know what he meant.

"Let go and haul, Tom," he said. "We'll be coming onto a new course, is all. Loose the mainsheet, I say, and make the most of it."

I searched through our chests and bags and makeshift boxes until I found the lamps and the oil. I arranged them in a way that lit every corner, then helped carry in our bits of furniture, and first of all the long settee so that my mother might have a place to lie as the work went on around her. It never bothered Father that she was such a shiftless thing, but it bothered me no end. I carried things until my arms were numb, hating that I had to do it. One day, I imagined, I would have a man whose only duty would be to carry my furniture about. "I should like the ottoman over there, James," I would say, pointing. And he would pick it up with a nod and a "Very well, Mr. Tin." I would have a gang of servants, a footman for my carriage. I would race through London in the smartest of curricles, with two of the finest horses. In every way, I would be better than Mr. Goodfellow.

That dream took a bit of a turn in the morning, when I started at my new school. Father would have said, "It damned near struck its colors."

The school had a grand name: Mr. Poppery's Academy for Boys. But it consisted entirely of the front room of the Poppery home, with a blackboard hung on a wall of bloodred paper, and six little chairs for the six fat boys. They were like pastry and lard, not one of them the picture of a young gentleman. Mr. Poppery himself looked like a small, homeless dog. He was thin and crooked, except for his right arm—nearly the size of a blacksmith's—with which he hammered his lessons into our backsides. We were to pay our tuition every day, dropping pennies into a wooden box as Mr. Poppery pretended to look aside. But on my first morning I hadn't a coin in my pocket, so I hung back, growing more and more distressed as the pennies chinked into the box. I was ready to pretend to drop one in, until Mr. Poppery covered the slot with his hand and told me in a whisper, with a wink, "It's taken care of, Master Tin."

It was a dismal school, and I hated it. But when my father came home from his business of waiting all day in the Admiralty, begging for the ship that was never his, when he brushed the soot from his shoulders and asked how my first day had gone, I lied. "Mr. Poppery's a fine fellow," I said. "He's got a topping school." I wasn't trying to spare my father's feelings. I was frightened that he would put me out to work or, even worse, send me off to sea.

He only nodded as he took off his coat. He reached it up to a hook at the door, and a pencil fell from his pocket. I bent down to get it, but Father pushed me away and snatched up the pencil himself. "Go see to your mother," he snapped.

He was seldom angry at me; I didn't understand why he acted that way. But I felt rather hurt, and didn't go in to see Mother. I went outside instead, to sit on our crooked little porch.

Already it was dark. It always was when Father came home in October. I looked up, surprised to see how many stars there were. It seemed that thousands had appeared where there had never been stars before. They filled the sky in a nearly solid spray of light, but over the city the fog gleamed thick and pale above all the lamps and lights that burned there. As I watched, it grew even thicker and taller. It came rolling over the farmyards, over the burying grounds and the old workhouse of St. Pancras. It filled up Camden Street and oozed across to Archer. It covered me up and swallowed the stars.

And in the foulness of its yellow cloak, I heard the tolling of a bell.

It was a strange sound in the fog, at once both faint and clear, both near and far away. It was such an unusual sound that it drew Father out beside me, and he said, "Good heavens!" when he saw how thick the fog had become. He listened to the bell with his head cocked. The sound was faint, yet strangely clear. "That's a passing bell," he said.

I knew what it was. Somewhere, maybe miles away, some poor fellow lay dying, and the bell marked the passing of his soul.

"A child," said Father, hearing the pattern of the chimes.

Then the telling strokes began, one for each year of that young person's life.

Inside the house, my mother's voice rose to a high warble. "There's no luck in hearing a passing bell," she said.

"No, nor harm," Father muttered beside me. But I felt a chill as the bell tolled on—eleven times, twelve—then only twice more. The child who was dying was the same age as me.

"No luck. No luck in that," shrilled Mother.

And she was right.

I FIND A DANGER AND A TREASURE

tuso

In the morning they came for my father. Two burly men, thick as tree stumps, marched him down the steps and into the fog. One at each side, pinning his elbows, they took him off to debtor's prison.

My mother wailed. She tried to stop them at the door, quivering in her black shawls. But the men only knocked her aside so rudely that my father roared, "Keep your filthy hands off her!" He struggled for a moment, until he saw that it was useless, then looked back as the men stepped him to the street.

"We're not beaten yet," he said. "We shall weather this blow, as we've weathered all others."

"Tell me what to do," I said.

His chin was turned fully to his shoulder. "You must find money, Tom," he told me.

"But how?" I called. "Father, how?"

Already he was graying into the fog. He had no answer. My mother sobbed as she held me. "It was the bell," she shouted. "It was the passing bell!"

"No," said Father, nearly gone now. "You see, Tom. This is what comes from crushing cockroaches."

I thought he was joking. I thought he was so brave to be making merry on his way to prison. But he was really talking about himself, as I learned a moment later. No sooner had he vanished completely into the awful fog—with a final round of oaths from the men, and the fading clatter of a horse's hoofs—than another man arrived.

His voice came first—"Ahoy the house!"—and that was all I needed to know. Only one man would speak those words in a voice like that.

Out of the fog came Mr. Goodfellow. He was dressed to the nines, in top hat and cape, and the one he tipped up and the other he flipped back as he came up the steps to our door. "Good day, Mrs. Tin," he said, with a nod to her. Me, he just ignored.

"What have you done to us now?" asked my mother.

"Why, you strike me to the quick, madam," said he. "I'm only trying to help."

She leapt at him. Her fingers curled, a snarl in her throat, she went up like a panther. But Mr. Goodfellow easily held her off. He was a strong man. He was bigger and stronger and richer than I or my father. In every way he was better.

"Now, listen," said Mr. Goodfellow. He held my mother by the wrist, and she folded up at his feet, down to her knees on the floor. "I have taken it upon myself to consolidate the debts of Mr. Tin. Everything he owes is henceforth owed to me, and a trifling amount it is."

"How much?" I asked. He didn't answer.

"How much?" asked Mother.

"Thirty-nine pounds," he said. "Thirty-nine pounds and a ha'penny, to be exact. But the latter I'll forgo."

His trifling amount was a princely sum to me. His ha'penny alone would buy me a muffin or a cold glass of raspberryade. The balance I could hardly imagine.

"A pittance," said Mr. Goodfellow, with a wave of his fingers. "However, I am prepared to forgo the *entire* amount if Mr. Tin will agree to work for Goodfellow and company."

"Is that what you want?" I asked. "Is that why you've hounded us for years, to get my father on your beastly ships?"

He looked at me, and then away. To him I wasn't worth a second glance.

Still on her knees, my mother stared up at him. Her face had once been pretty, but it hadn't seen the sun since Kitty's death, and now was ashy white. "How dare you, sir?" she asked. "Weren't you brave enough to come while he was here?"

"Madam . . . ," he said.

"How dare you?" Mother said again, in a voice that had no fire. She managed to gather some dignity as she picked herself up and rose beside him, small and frail. "You've ruined us, sir," she said. "All for revenge, for a wound on your pride."

"The whys and wherefores are between myself and Mr. Tin," said he. "But let me tell you, madam: ruined you shall be unless your husband agrees to my terms."

He tipped his hat again and backed from the door. I swallowed, looking straight at him. "*I* will go," I said.

"No!" cried Mother.

But I ignored her. "I will go in my father's place," I told him, trembling at my courage. I thought I might faint if he

11

took me up on my bargain. As he looked back at me, I resigned myself to a short life and an early death on the sea that I feared.

But his only answer was a laugh, a hearty laugh that shook him all over and made those cold eyes twinkle.

It was worse than if he had said no. I had offered him my life, and it angered me to be so utterly belittled.

"I insist," I said.

He laughed even harder. "Oh, you insist," he said, and snickered. "I need a *man,* young Master Tin. Why, you wouldn't last a day, not an hour, on the sea. You belong at Mr. Poppery's, boy. I've seen to it that your tuition has been paid for a year. It's already a portion of your father's debt."

I turned and ran away. Consumed with shame, with hate, I couldn't bear to face the man a moment longer. I retreated to the parlor, scampering down the hall like one of the cockroaches I had startled there. I heard Mr. Goodfellow's laugh, and then his voice telling my mother, "I'll expect to hear from you directly." The door closed, and I heard his fine leather boots taking him down through the fog.

My mother followed me into the parlor. I was looking at the few little things we owned, but I was really seeing those that were gone. The sword that my father had accepted from a surrendering Frenchman; where was that? His medals were gone, and his best braided hat. His charts and his tools and his pilot books; all of them were gone. For the first time I wondered about the pennies that had gone to the tollbooth, and exactly where they had come from. And then I thought about my school tuition, and I groaned. Why had I never seen what was happening? My father, in selling nearly everything he owned, had sold *himself* along with his sailorly things.

"It's worth any price to spare you from going to sea," said my mother, as though she had read my mind. "I never should have married a sailor, and I won't have one for a son. You're to be a gentleman, Tom."

I saw what despair had been brought to that end, and I vowed to set things straight. I marched to the hall. I began pulling on my shoes, my good gleaming shoes that might have cost my father his sextant.

"Where are you going?" asked Mother.

I bent over to tie the laces. Frayed and knotted, they seemed shamefully shabby in such fine shoes. The money I'd been given to buy laces had bought me a Chelsea bun.

"Tell me where," she said. "Are you going to sea? Tom, you're not running away to sea, are you?" Mother took my arm. "There's no future there; only death waits on the sea."

"Let me go," I said, pulling easily from her grasp. "I have to settle accounts."

I didn't know what I would do or where I would go. But I was certain that I couldn't leave my father in a debtor's prison. I took my coat from its hook. Then—I didn't know why—I put it back and took my father's instead. Perhaps I thought his coat would make me a man. Perhaps I wanted him to hold me, and since his real arms weren't there to do it, I would have to wrap myself in the woolen ones that smelled so much of him.

I put on the coat; I opened the door.

Mother tried to slam it shut. "Tom, don't go," she said.

"Mother, please." I moved her aside and stepped out to the porch.

"No son of mine will ever go to sea," she said. "Tom, if you walk away now I have no son."

"Please don't worry," I told her. I kissed her on the cheek, then hurried off before I could change my mind, before my courage deserted me. I ran into the fog, and her cries came with me.

"I have no son," she shouted in her madwoman's screech. "Do you hear me? I have no son!"

I ran as fast and far as I could. I ran though my ribs felt stitched together, though my lungs wheezed. From street to street, through a churchyard and a field, I ran on and on. I passed ghostly houses, ghostly trees, coughing globs of phlegm, thick and yellow, as though it were bits of the fog I was retching from my body.

I knew London only from the Surrey side, as a panorama of spires and domes along the curve of the Thames. To come at it from the north, so blindly that I couldn't see more than thirty paces, left me hopelessly confused.

The streets twisted and turned and stopped altogether. Along them milled people and carts and carriages, more and more as I went along, until sometimes the street was choked from side to side. All slowly appeared and slowly faded, as though I'd come to a city full of phantoms, a drowned Atlantis in the watery fog. From the gloom and the shadows, an endless assortment of odd-looking hawkers reached out to sell me their wares. I was offered pocket glasses and seashells, birds' nests and coal, sponges, spoons, and a clarinet. I stumbled through a market full of street-sellers, each shouting about the thing he was selling, in such a babble of "Fish!" and "Potatoes!" and "Whelks!" and "Hot eels!" that it made not the slightest sense.

But the smells of the food were strong and enticing. I stopped in the middle of the crowd and felt through the pockets of my father's coat, hoping to find a farthing. But all I brought out was a fistful of pencils with their sharpened ends jammed into a little tin cup. I stared at them for a moment, until I suddenly felt tears come to my eyes. A picture formed, clear as a sunny day, of my father pausing on these same streets, hawking his pencils to raise the pennies that sent me to school.

For a minute or more I stood in the swirling crowd, nearly weeping at the sadness of it, knowing that if Mr. Goodfellow suddenly emerged beside me, I would thrust those pencils through his coat, through his breast, and pierce his black heart. Then a hand reached out and stole the pencils. Another, perhaps the same, stole the cup.

That was nearly the end for me. I would have gone straight home if I had known which way to walk. But the crowd had turned me around so that I didn't know east from west, or scarcely up from down. I tried to stop a peddler and ask him for directions, but he only went rattling along with his little cart and his tiny donkey, crying out, "Buy, buy, buy! Buy a bonnet, buy a bootlace!"

I set off through another maze of streets, past another row of shops. Then I arrived suddenly at a set of stairs, and at their bottom was the muddy bank of the Thames. I had blundered right past the City.

I sat on the stone step. Cold and hungry, desperately alone, I decided to wait for the fog to thin. I pulled my collars tight, linked my hands inside my cuffs, and watched an old man trudging through the mud below me.

He was gray and grizzled; he was blind. His eyes were wrapped with a black cloth tied behind his head, its long tails drooping to his shoulders. On his back hung a tattered bag that was clotted with mud at the bottom, as though he had set it down and picked it up a hundred thousand times. He carried a crooked stick that he poked deep in the mud. I heard the squelching, sucking sound it made each time he pulled it out.

I was used to seeing mud larks combing the riversides for their bits of bone and glass and iron, for anything they could sell. But always they'd been children; I had never seen an old, blind man at the game.

He was a master at it. He stepped and poked, stepped and poked, like a huge and ragged heron. His feet were bare, his trousers rolled to his knees, and his long coat scraped on the mud, smoothing behind him each puckered mound left by his stick.

Suddenly he bent down. The bag fell from his shoulders. His hands went into the mud, to his wrists, to his elbows. He dug like a dog, splashing the mud across his legs and his coat. He pulled out a black blob that grew smaller and smaller as he shook the mud away, until he was left with a little disk—a coin that he put between his teeth and bit, hard, on one side. Then into his sack it went, and up he got to start again.

I envied him then, as old and blind as he was. I took off my shoes, fumbling with the tangled laces. I peeled away my socks and stuffed them inside. I tied the laces together and hung the shoes around my neck, then started down the steps.

The stone was bitterly cold, the mud even colder. It felt thick as treacle, and bottomless; my foot vanished into it. Each step was a struggle, and I managed only half a dozen before the mud gripped me like glue. I nearly fell forward, crying out as I tried to catch my balance.

The blind man's head went up. "Who's there?" he asked, his voice a croak, an ugly "grawk" that made him seem more birdlike than ever.

He scared me with his quickness and his tattered clothes, the way his head swung round to listen. Surrounded by the fog, with the river flowing by, I was in the loneliest place of all. The city existed only as a hum of noise, a jumble of gray shapes piled atop the weed-covered stones and steps. The river was a band of darkness fading into yellow. It was creeping toward me, I saw, as I stood there with my breath bated. It came licking over the mud, around the shallow domes that cockles had made. It stretched out twisting fingers that darted toward me with amazing speed, through the hollows and ripples.

The water scared me more than the blind man did. I imagined myself stuck where I was, fixed to the mud like a bug on fresh paint, as the river rose and covered me. I saw myself underwater, swaying to and fro with the current, my arms writhing over my head.

My fear got the better of me. I decided that nothing that might be hidden in the mud was worth the effort it took just to stand there, with water oozing at my feet. Desperate to reach the bank again, I turned a clumsy half circle, and there was the blind man in front of me. With the mud so thick, I couldn't run. I tried to move quietly, but the black goo kissed at my shins and my ankles. My shoes, swinging on their laces, thumped against my coat.

"Who's there?" the blind man said again. "This is my bit of river. What's in it is mine."

His face was turned right toward me now. His stick went into the mud, his knee rose, and he swung around as slick as an eel. He came squelching toward me, oozing along the riverbank.

I took another step, suddenly terrified that the fog might thicken and hide the stairs that led to safety. I tried to struggle forward, but only fell back, and the blind man came closer.

I used my hands to lift my feet, hauling on the rolled bundles of my trouser legs. I pulled up and stepped forward, then shouted in surprise and pain as I trod upon a thing as sharp as a knife. I tottered sideways and collapsed.

"Get off my river," said the blind man in his croaking voice. He stepped along through the mud.

My ankle was twisted painfully. I felt along the bones, along skin that was now gritty, down to my ankle. Then I felt the thing I'd stood on, something hard and sharp, and it very nearly filled my fist as I pulled it out.

I could scarcely believe what I saw. Only half enclosed by my fingers, stained by a sheen of mud, was a diamond. It might have been the largest diamond the world had ever known. It caught the yellow light of the fog and turned it to a deep and amber glow. My heart leapt to see it.

And then the blind man was upon me.

three
THE BONE PICKER'S JOURNEY

The blind man bowled me down. I fell flat on my back, and he sprang on my chest, straddling it with his knees. We wrestled in the mud of the riverbank as the water rose toward us. The blind man's fingers gripped my leg and then my arm.

"What did you take?" he croaked. "Give it to me! It's mine."

I tried to squirm out from under him. I kicked with both legs and punched with one arm, but I held on to the diamond as tightly as I could.

"You devil," he said. "You thief."

I put all my strength into one hard push. I bucked up against the blind man, tipping him sideways. He lost his grip on my arm, but he didn't fall away. His hands flew straight to my throat. He found my shoes hanging there, then the laces round my neck, and he twisted those tight in a moment.

The string cut against me, the little knots biting into sinews, closing off my throat. I looked up at the blind man's face, at a mouth of rotten teeth snarling below the bandage. I saw my own hand flailing at his shoulder, as though it belonged to someone else. I thought the fog was turning red, that bright stars and blotches of black were floating through it. But I still held on to my diamond.

The blind man twisted the shoes round and round. I couldn't breathe in and couldn't breathe out; I couldn't fight back anymore. The rising river touched my feet, then rushed into the hollowed mud all along my body. It chilled my legs, my spine, and shoulders all at once, and it turned my fear to utter terror.

Everything I could see turned to red and gray and then to black. I felt my hands fall to my sides. Then I heard a snapping sound that seemed loud as a gunshot. I was sure that a vessel had burst in my body, and I was almost glad that my end had come.

But the blind man cried out the most terrible oaths. I saw the world brighten, and felt my breaths rushing in and out, my lungs pumping like a blacksmith's bellows. I saw the blind man clearly again, ugly and mud-spotted. In his hands were my shoes, the broken ends of the laces dangling. Too knotted, too frayed, they had snapped in the middle.

I raised the diamond in my hand. I brought it up as swiftly and powerfully as I could, and I clouted the blind man on the back of his head. Black spit flew from his mouth.

I hit him again, and again after that. With each blow, the blind man grunted and swore. Then I hit him once more, and he toppled sideways. The water was halfway over my ribs, and it floated me out from the hollow, out from the grip of the mud. I feared that it would float me completely away, down past the city and out to the sea. I struggled like a flounder toward the stairs, then used the stones to haul myself upright.

I looked back then, expecting to see the blind man facedown in the water. But already he was on his hands and knees, groping for his stick and his bag. His head was lifted, the bandage flapping, and I sensed that he knew exactly where I was.

I turned and ran. I mounted the stairs and dashed down the streets. At every corner I turned in a different direction, hoping to find a busy street or a marketplace. I wanted a crowd to hide among, or at the very least a poor parish Charlie who might save me. I would have to hope I didn't scare the wits from him, for I must have looked a horror. I had no shoes, no socks, a coat that was clotted with mud. But the streets seemed empty.

Chilled to the bone, I stopped at last in a narrow alley, below a lamp that cast a halo in the fog. I drew the diamond from my pocket and saw it gleam and sparkle. I knew that I held in the span of my fingers a wealth greater than Mr. Goodfellow's entire fortune. I held my father's freedom from prison, the relief forever of all his worries. I held his own ship, if that was what he wanted, a mansion for us in the country, my own curricle, and a pacer for Sunday rides. Footmen and butlers and scullery maids danced across the faces of that diamond. Right then, in its glow, I learned the meaning of greed.

But a sound pulled me out of my wild dreams. Not far away, somewhere in the fog, I thought I heard the blind man's stick tapping at the stones. I stayed where I was, pressed between the lamppost and the wall. The man had ears but not eyes, and I hoped he would pass me by.

The taps and creaks came closer.

Then out of the fog came a horse. It stepped along with

an unusual gait, as though in a slowed-down canter. Its shoulders rolling, its head bobbing high, it was the strangest horse I'd ever seen. A straw hat was tied over its ears, and a glistening blanket covered its back. But strangest of all, it had a wooden leg.

I laughed to see it, from sheer relief. The wooden leg—at its left front—hit the stones with a thump. The three good hoofs pattered after it, then the wooden leg swung forward and tapped again.

The blanket was a coat for the horse, a ragamuffin's coat made of patches of leather and silk and tartan. It was hung every inch with shells and bones, with bits of tin and curls of copper wire. A steam came off it from the horse's sweat, and whispering rustles and jingles. Behind the horse appeared a wagon, and then its driver—a bone grubber, he looked—sitting on a rickety seat. He wore the top hat and mourning coat of a grubber, both slick and bright with grease.

The horse saw me first. It shimmied away with a funny, strangled cry. Then the driver looked straight at me, and his hand went up toward his heart. His hat fell off. It bounced on his knee, on the wagon wheel, and landed right before me, spinning on its brim. Underneath the hat, he wore a dark cloth wrapped like a hood round his head.

"By jabers!" he said. "Are you trying to give me apoplexy, boy?" He shook his head. "Come out from there, young nasty-man."

I slid from behind the post, holding my diamond in a coat pocket.

"You're wet. And you're muddy," said the bone grubber. "What are you up to, boy?"

"Nothing, sir," I said.

"Wal-*ker!*" he said, an expression I'd heard from many lips, but never from a grubber's.

"You're on the tidy dodge, ain't you?" he said. "You're appealin' to the mercies of the ladies, that's what you're doing. You're on the touch, ain't you?"

"No, sir." I didn't even know what he meant.

"Walker!" he said again. "I know your type."

He seemed gruff but harmless, a bear of a man who looked even bigger in a coat too small. It stretched across his shoulders and bulged at his arms, as though the stitching could pop at any moment.

"Well, ain't you going to pick up me hat?" he said. "Seeing as you knocked it from me head."

I stooped down and got it.

"What's your name?"

"Tom Tin, sir," I said, holding up the hat. It was so foul and greasy that it stuck to my fingers.

"I'm Worms," he said. "And it ain't *Mister* Worms neither. Just Worms is all."

He reached down and took the hat. He secured it on his head, twisting its brim until it fell into place. "Well, Tom Tin," he asked. "Have you a penny in your pocket?"

"No, sir," I said. "Not a penny." *Only a diamond,* I thought. *Only a king's fortune.*

"Have you eaten today?"

I shook my head.

"Ohhhh," he groaned. "I should be killed for my kindness. But come up, boy, and I'll feed you."

At any other time I would have turned away from the fellow without a word. Filthy, likely homeless, he was too far beneath me to waste the time of day upon. But I was desperate to leave the haunts of the blind man, and more famished than I'd known. I climbed up into his wagon, amused to think that I, so rich, could eat the scraps of one so poor. One day, I thought, I would reward him for his act, just to see the delight

23

on his ugly old face. I would seek him out when I'd sold my diamond, and give him a new topper, a new horse with the proper number of legs. Then, one far-off day, I would sit in the finest club with the finest fellows, and oh, how they would laugh to hear I had once dined with a ragpicker.

I settled beside him on the seat. All the things he had found were arranged in boxes behind it. There were bones of all sizes. There were white rags and colored rags, a box of broken pottery, another of bits of tin. There was a box of horse manure and a box of dog droppings, and a small box, quite ornate, that was full of the ragged tips of old cigars. Together, it all made a stench that I couldn't believe.

Worms turned around on the seat and rummaged among the boxes. "First thing, a blanket," he said, pulling one up. It was gray and worn, and likely crawling with lice, but I felt better to have it wrapped around me.

"There, lad." He patted it into place, smiled, and patted again. "Now let's find you some belly-timber."

His hands were black with dirt. I remembered my mother telling me that she could grow potatoes in the dirt under my fingernails. Worms could have wallowed pigs under his.

"Ah, some cheese," he said. "That will grease your gills."

It was moldy, I saw when he brought it out in his fist. He gave me that, and a toe of bird-picked bread, and a lump of green mutton falling from its bone. I tried to eat without chewing, without tasting, without looking at Worms, who grinned through his hood and watched till I finished. "That hit the spot?" he said, then clucked his tongue. "Start up, Peggy."

The three-legged horse pulled at its harness, jolting the wagon forward. We rumbled along into the fog, and all the little decorations swayed and rattled on the horse's many-colored coat.

"What happened to its leg?" I asked.

"Oh, I et it," said Worms, with a pleasant smile.

I was happy to be with him as the wagon carried me away from the river. My diamond in my pocket, my life of riches ahead, I was quite content to ride for a while with the grubber. But I was careful to keep a hand on my pocket, and to do nothing that might make him think I had something of value.

The horse swung to the right and suddenly stopped by a heap of old ash. Worms picked up a stick at least twelve feet long. I expected him to beat the poor horse, but he only jabbed an end of the stick into the ashes. He grunted and muttered, then turned the stick neatly around with the same sort of flourish a drum major would make with a fancy baton. A little basket was tied to the stick, and Worms pushed it into the rubbish and turned it all about. The three-legged horse watched him.

A few moments of fishing and the bone grubber hauled in his catch: a tiny bottle with a cork; three inches of wire bent in the shape of a Q. Into the boxes went his treasures; into the wagon went his long stick. "Right-o, Peggy," he said, and we started off again.

Worms brushed soot and ashes from his knee. "Where are you going?" he asked.

"To the City," I said.

"Back on the tidy dodge, is it?" He winked. "Or pick a pocket, perhaps?"

"No, sir," I told him.

"Well, of course you will. What else are you to do?" The wagon stopped and Worms took up his stick. "Who hasn't given a cove a tumble now and then?" He tilted the stick up high and poked it into a dustbin. "I got me start that way meself, before I became a man of means."

I smiled at that, to think he imagined he was rich. I decided that I would give him a bucketful of guineas, just to teach him what riches were.

He brought in the bowl of a clay pipe and a bit of cigar the size of his thumb. This last delighted him no end. He looked like a boy on Christmas morning, his eyes shining.

"You remind me of him," said Worms as we rumbled along again.

"Who?"

"Of *meself*," he said sharply. "That boy I was then. The future before me. I done well, Tom Tin."

"I see that," I said.

"Yes, it's a fine life I've got. There's not a bit of Spital-fields I haven't seen between old Peggy's ears." He clucked fondly at the horse. "I been to Trinity Square, out to Woolwich and the Medway now and then to fetch the ones from the ships—and that's a long haul for a three-legged horse, let me tell you. Oh, the things I see. It's a fine life, right enough."

"I'm envious," I said, and he beamed.

"Tell you what, my boy. I'll give you what no one gave me. A leg up, young Tom." He turned to smile upon me from the darkness of his hood. "I'll give you tuppence for a night's work. Two big pennies for your very own."

I laughed. Tuppence was nothing to me anymore. But I needed something to tide me over until I found my father. I had no idea how to sell a diamond on my own. "Well, thank you, Worms," I said.

All evening I rode with the bone grubber, from one rubbish heap to the next. The river water soaked from my clothes to the blanket, and a steam came up from that, just as it did from the horse. For the blind man I spared no more thought. I fell asleep to the sounds and motions of the wagon, and dreamed of being rich. I drove through London in a cabriolet pulled by thirty horses. They ran abreast as I dashed along the Mall, as people skittled from my path. When I woke, the fog had cleared, and the nighttime sky shone with stars. The wagon wasn't moving, and I was all alone.

Peggy stood beside a stone wall and a grim old church. Her ears, poking through slits in her straw hat, fluttered and twitched. Then I heard what she had heard, old Worms calling out in a harsh whisper from beyond the wall, "Tom Tin. Tom Tin."

I got down and went through the gate to the churchyard. For a moment, the sight of the crosses and tombstones brought back the memory of fetching my mother from a place just the same. Then Worms whispered again, and I saw him on my right. In the blackness of the graves he shimmered in a strange, unnatural light. It glowed on his chest and his hands, as though he stood before a fire that wasn't there. Then he stooped, reached *into* the ground, and brought up a lantern, which he held high.

His coat and hat had been tossed atop a gravestone. All around him, the grass of the churchyard had been torn up and turned over. There was a pile of dirt, and a pile of sod, and Worms in the middle, beckoning with his hand. "Hurry, Tom," he whispered.

I walked toward him, between the graves. I saw a shovel lying atop the dirt, and finally made sense of it all.

Worms had dug a shaft straight down through a grave, and now stood over the opening, pointing.

"Look in there," he whispered. "You won't believe your eyes."

four
INTO THE GRAVE

I didn't look right away into the open grave. Worms was smiling at me, and globs of dirt were falling from his hands. They landed with plops and tiny thuds, and went rolling into the gaping shaft.

"You were sleeping so tight I didn't want to wake you," he said in a low voice. "But don't worry, Tom Tin, you'll still get your tuppence. The work ain't finished yet."

I didn't care about the work, nor about the tuppence.

"Take a look, Tom. Quick," he said.

The lantern bobbed toward the grave. The shadows of the tombstones swooped hugely across the wall of the silent church.

"You're a grave robber," I said.

"Shhh!" he whispered. "No, I ain't that, Tom. I don't touch their rings, their pennies, or nothing. I'm a resurrection man. It's the bodies I'm after, and look at this one, Tom. Look down there."

He reached out and grabbed my arm. He pulled me forward, and I was certain that he was going to tip me into that open grave. He was going to put me in it and cover me over, and why I couldn't imagine. Then I thought of my diamond. Had he found it while I slept? But there it was in my pocket. I could feel its hardness through the cloth.

Worms pulled harder. I stumbled over his shovel, right to the edge of the hole. Suddenly I was bending over the shaft he'd made, looking down at a body in a coffin, at the shape of a corpse's head.

Only the top bit of the coffin was open, the wood shattered away. As Worms lowered his lantern, the light flashed onto the pale face of a dead boy. There were dark coins on his eyes, a handkerchief tied below his chin. But the boy didn't seem dead at all. He seemed to be playing a pretending game down there in the earth.

Worms scrambled into the grave. He brushed the coins away and pulled the handkerchief off. Then he pressed himself against the earth, so that I might see past him. He smiled up at me as I stared down. "Now, that's what I call a dead ringer," he said.

It was true that I couldn't believe my eyes. It was as though I were staring into a well and seeing my own reflection in the water. The boy in the coffin was *exactly* like me. He might have been my age to the very day. The passing bell that had rung in the fog must have been tolling for him.

"Pass me the rope there, Tom," said Worms.

It lay on the other side of the hole like a coiled snake. I wondered how many bodies it had hauled from the ground.

"Hurry, Tom," said Worms in his low voice. He was crouching now over the broken coffin, ready to slip the dead boy out by his shoulders. "We're goners if we're caught geaching here like this."

I could have left him there and run away. Why I didn't I would never know, though I would often wish I had. But I'd always done just what I was told, and now I did it again. I went to fetch the rope; I bent to pick it up. Then the ground gave way at the grave's edge, and down I went. I scrambled for something to stop me, but all I could grab was the rope, and it slithered in on top of me. I landed on the coffin. The diamond in my pocket thumped against the wood, and I lay face to face with my dead twin. I gathered breath to scream.

Worms clamped his hand on my mouth. "Easy, Tom," he said. "Keep your wits about you, now."

He pulled me upright, suddenly not so kind. "Clumsy fool," he called me. "You stay here and *I'll* go up. And take off your coat if you don't want to smell like a graveyard."

He did it for me in his anger, pulling it from my shoulders, flinging it onto the earth. Then he used me for a ladder, and his boots dug at my thighs, my chest, my shoulders before he rolled away into the starlight. I bent down to get my coat, but his head came back above me, and he snapped at me to leave it there. "Put the rope around him, Tom. Quick! Under his shoulders, now, his *shoulders,* boy!"

I didn't want to stay in that grave an instant longer than I had to. So I gritted my teeth and threaded the rope below the dead boy's shoulders, though my skin crawled to do it.

"Tie a knot. Make a noose," growled Worms.

I wished I had listened when my father had tried to teach me bowlines and sheet bends and whatnot. Twice I dropped the rope, and twice I stooped to pick its coils from the dead boy's chest. "A noose. A noose," said Worms, but all I managed was a great tangle.

"Now lift him up, boy."

The rope went tight as Worms started pulling. I straddled the dead boy, my feet in his coffin, and scooped my hands below his shoulders. I pulled, and up he sat, his head nodding forward, his mouth gaping open. He seemed to slide himself from the ground, standing on legs that had no muscles, swinging arms that could do no work. He wrapped them round my waist, then around my ribs. Clods of earth tumbled as he slithered up the side of his grave as though to his resurrection. He was dressed in a good shirt and a fine long coat, but his feet were bare. They were white, pathetic things to see as they went sliding past me.

I had tipped my head, and was watching him rise to the light and the sky when my knots unraveled and down he came.

He fell into my arms, and I into his, and we leaned together in a cold embrace against the grave's sheer wall. His chin hit my shoulder, and his teeth chattered shut. I thought that my mind, like my mother's, might unhinge at the horror.

"Stop mucking about," said Worms. "Give him a boost."

I gained a strength from my fear and desperation. I ducked a shoulder under the boy, and straightened him up toward Worms. He rose quickly then, slipping face-first from his grave to the ground. His legs swung stiffly above me for a moment, until they too slid across the stars. His white toes scraped at the earth, and then he was gone.

I didn't have time to move. Worms reached down, grabbed my shoulder, and hauled me up beside him. He stripped the clothes from the dead boy, rolling the body over and over as he pulled away the coat and the shirt and left them in a heap. Then the body, white and naked in the starlight, lay atop another grave. "Take his feet," said Worms.

We carried the boy to the street, past old Peggy to the

back of the wagon. Worms reached underneath and worked some sort of latch. Then he pulled out a hidden shelf, revealing another body, a boy as naked as the first, but not quite whole. Squirms of maggots filled his eyes.

Onto the shelf went my twin. Worms pushed it shut. "Up on the seat," he told me.

"My coat," I cried.

"Get up there and wait." He gave me a push. "If a Charlie comes round, you whistle, you hear?"

Worms went scurrying back to the graveyard. I heard his shovel clang and scrape, his breath gasp in fierce grunts. Again I thought of running away, but now I would lose my diamond. Too frightened to join him, I sat and waited, fretting on the wagon, staring up and down the street. When at last he came out he was dressed again in coat and top hat, carrying his shovel and his lantern, and my own coat beneath his arm. He opened the drawer and threw the shovel inside. The lantern he hung on a hook, the coat he tossed to me.

I felt right away for the diamond. I turned the coat over and over on my knees, patting every inch of it. But it all flattened across my trousers, and just as I realized the diamond was gone, I saw that it wasn't my coat at all.

"This is the dead boy's," I said.

"I know it," said Worms, climbing up beside me. "Better than yours by half. Why, Tom Tin, this is your lucky day."

My heart sank. My riches were gone, my bubbles burst. I couldn't tell Worms why I suddenly sobbed one heartbroken cry. He thought that his gesture of kindness had pleased me. So he patted my shoulder and gathered his reins. "Put it on," he said. "Let's see how splendid you look."

I thrust my arms through the sleeves; I hauled the coat around me.

"Like royalty," he said. "The duke of Shoreditch sure enough." He set his hat straight and wriggled his bottom onto the seat. "Move along, Peggy."

As we drew away from the graveyard, I looked back. If there was any thought in my mind of leaving Worms and returning right then to that place, it was dashed on the instant. Worms closed his fingers round my arm and told me, "Sit tight. We're into this together now."

I would have to return to the churchyard on the next dark night, armed with my own shovel and lamp. So I studied the route we took, counting every corner, memorizing every building. I tried to use the lessons of my schooling and invent a rhyme that I might easily remember. *Left at the blacking house, right at the sewer drain. Left at the corner and right once again.* The verses piled up in my head until I had something nearly as long as the *Iliad*, and just as likely to be forgotten.

Peggy's wooden leg tapped and banged. The wagon lurched along Tyburn Road, and I thought of the dead boy who rode in the back, behind and below me. I thought of him shaking and trembling, cuddling up to that more loathesome thing at his side. Then we wheeled sharply left into a dark alley, and I ducked my head to pass below a great wooden boot that hung from a shoemaker's shop.

I looked back at it, thinking I had found the landmark that might lead me again to the diamond. *Right at the boot, to the Tyburn route,* I told myself.

Peggy wheezed and panted, and Worms brought her to a stop. "Here we are," he said. "Now, you're about to meet a gentleman, Tom, a right and proper gent. So mind your p's and q's."

"You know a gentleman?" I asked, surprised.

"Wal-ker!" said Worms. "I know many of 'em, Tom, and this one's a dandy. Rubs shoulders with lords, he does—with the finest men in London. A genuine doctor, he is." Worms tugged lightly at my sleeve. "Good thing you've got a fine new coat."

We were not in the sort of place where a gentleman would live. The street was sloped, narrow, almost evil in its darkness. Somewhere a baby cried, and a woman laughed hysterically. But the buildings looked abandoned, every window dark save for one. A single candle flickered in a little pane below the street, down a flight of stairs.

Worms set his hat straight. He adjusted his hood, and wiped his hands on his coat. "Look sharp, Tom," he said. "The street arabs will steal you blind here. They'll slice your throat for a farthing."

I watched him go—so shabby, but thinking himself so grand—straight toward the one lit window, down the steps as though into the ground. I decided that the moment he went inside, I would take his shovel and head back to the grave-yard. I was afraid to go alone, but afraid to stay as well; I scarcely knew which was worse. The street arabs scared me, but so did old Worms. I wanted my father, and I wanted my diamond.

Worms knocked on the door. The sound echoed up and down, back and forth.

I climbed down very casually and strolled to the rear of the wagon. I hadn't seen exactly how Worms had opened the drawer, so I leaned against the wood and furtively felt for the latch. In the stairwell, chains rattled and bolts creaked open. A light spilled out that wasn't much brighter than the candle. I stretched up on my toes, curious to see who would keep such a mysterious place.

It was a mysterious man, of course. Dressed for the city,

in a cape and a ruffled shirt, he had a beard like the devil's—black and pointed—but wildly unkempt hair. He seemed surprised to find Worms on his doorstep, though there was little wonder at that. "Oh, Lord, not you," he said. "Not now."

"Wal-ker! That's a fine welcome," said Worms.

The doctor peered past him, craning his neck. "I'm on my way out."

"I see that," said Worms. "To the rat fights, is it?"

"To the *opera*," said the doctor, reaching his hands across the doorway.

"Take him in," I whispered, as though I could will the doctor to open his door. I wanted Worms out of sight when I took his shovel and fled up the street. My hand groped below the wagon. I found something thick and bent that moved when I pulled on it. But when no latch clicked open, I realized that I was only tugging on the dead boy's toe.

"A cab is coming," the doctor told Worms. "It will arrive any moment. My friends are . . . They're important people. It wouldn't do for them to see you here."

"Oh, it wouldn't *do*," said Worms. "Walker!"

"Well, what have you brought?" snapped the doctor.

"A good-looking boy," said Worms. "Fresh as a daisy, and another besides."

My fingers brushed over slats and bars. Something moved, something rumbled, and the drawer lurched open. The boy's feet came out, white and sickly-looking. Beside them was the shovel, but I had no chance to take it.

"Fetch them in," the doctor said. "But hurry."

Worms came back at a run. Though large and heavy, he came so quickly that he caught me with the shelf pulled open. He stood and stared down, then raised his eyes to me. "Do you want all the world to see?" he asked.

He took the newly dead boy, my naked double, up on his

shoulders, then pushed the drawer with his hip. It locked itself shut as Worms went off again at the same lumbering trot, with the dead boy riding him backward, slapping at his hips. Then, before he even reached the foot of the steps, a carriage came rumbling up the street behind me. It was the doctor's cab, a big four-wheeler pulled by gray horses.

It startled old Peggy. She rapped her wooden leg on the street and tugged at the wagon. I didn't know if a three-legged horse could bolt, but I was afraid she would try. I ran up to her head and took hold of the bridle as the cab came to a stop just behind the wagon. Its door flung open, but I didn't see the man who stepped out. I didn't *need* to see him to know who it was.

"Ahoy the house!" he shouted.

Mr. Goodfellow. So Worms was right; his doctor friend *did* hobnob with the best. But what fate had brought him here, to the dingiest part of the city? I pressed myself against Peggy, thinking how much it would please Mr. Goodfellow to see me here, shoeless, minding a bone grubber's wagon.

"Ahoy the house!" he shouted again. He passed the wagon; he passed the horse on its other side, then stood facing the door. "Kingsley!" he called. "Kingsley, you fool."

A second man spilled from the cab, laughing as though Mr. Goodfellow were the greatest wit. "You'll have to fetch him out, Goody," he said. "Kingsley always keeps us waiting."

"Part of his charm." Mr. Goodfellow cupped his hands to his mouth and bellowed, "Kingsley!"

The pair had been into the gin, I could see. They wobbled their way across the street and down the steps. Just as they went in through the front, old Worms came scuttling from the back. He climbed onto the wagon and snatched up his reins.

"Walker!" he grumbled. "Who does he think he is, that

doctor? Blimey! Who does he *think he is*?" Worms shook his head. " 'Wait outside,' he tells me. Well, dash it, Tom, there's other doctors. Peas in pods they may be, but there's one around the corner here."

I sat up beside him, and Peggy hauled us along. Her head shaking, her breath snorting, she lurched up the hill at her steady pace. We rolled along through a dreary slum, splashing our wheels in gutters that ran with sewage. It was late enough that the streets were empty, bright enough that I could see rats feasting on the bits of horse droppings the finders had missed. On either side stood the lowest of lodging houses, their long windows turned to grimy checkerboards by all the squares of paper and wood that filled the missing panes. Dismal homes of dismal people, they were the haunts of thieves and waifs and crossing sweepers, the sorts of places where I was doomed to land myself if Mr. Goodfellow had his way, if I couldn't recover my diamond.

Suddenly, Worms looked around. "What was that?" he asked.

I had heard nothing but our own squeaks and taps. But old Worms seemed frightened. "Listen," he said.

And I heard it then.

Voices, high and eerie. They rose from my right, and then from my left, voices so faint and ghostly that the skin prickled on my neck. They came from behind and came from ahead, and a drumming began, like an army marching, as one of the arabs beat along dustbins. I saw others swirl into the street behind us, a mob of black in ragged clothes.

"Worms," I said. "Look!"

He glanced back only once, only for an instant, then thrashed at his reins. "Gee up, Peggy!" he shouted. "Run, you blessed glue pot!"

The poor old horse gave out a startled, strangled cry. Its

breath came in a great puff and a wheeze, and the wooden leg tapped faster. I looked back and saw the street arabs running, more rushing in behind them, one with a torch that flickered a red flame on bare shoulders and chests, in the empty windows of the lodging houses.

The wagon jolted over cobblestones. Peggy's leg tapped amid the clatter of her hoofs.

"She can't pull us both," said Worms, thrashing with the reins. "Get off, Tom!"

He tried to push me from the seat, but I clung to my place. "Here!" he shouted. "Take your tuppence and go."

He wrestled the money from his pocket and shoved it at my side. He pushed hard, and violently, and I grabbed for his wrists to save myself. I caught him by the hand. But his fingers, slick and greasy, slipped through my fist. The pennies fell into my palm, and I went tumbling from the wagon.

For an instant I thought that the wheel would crush my life away. But I bounced from the turning rim, and struck my head on the cobblestones.

five
AMONG THE URCHINS

The dead boy came after me. Down the streets and through the alleys, his feet pattered on paving stones, on cobbles and bricks. His arms held out, his eyes wide open, he shambled behind me through gardens and graveyards. Every time I looked back he was closer. And finally, at the Hungerford Stairs, I felt his hand on my shoulder.

I woke with a start from a terrible dream. With a gasp I sat bolt upright—just as the dead boy had sprung up in my nightmare. With my heart a-shudder I breathed deep breaths.

There was a boy beside me. His hand had been on my shoulder, but now it flew off, and he cried out in alarm— "Oh, Jeminy!"—to see me come awake so suddenly.

He was nearly as gruesome as the running corpse of my nightmare. His head was odd-shaped, his face rather twisted, his ears just lumps of flesh. He wore no shirt, only trousers that had frayed nearly to the knees, and just one suspender to hold them up. His ribs stuck out in turns and knobs, as though an old man's knuckled fingers clutched him below his skin.

"Look at him now," he said. "See there? Told you it's him."

"It ain't," said a black-haired fellow. "That's his coat, Penny, sure as a gun, but it ain't the Smasher."

I touched the back of my head. There was a lump as big as my fist, and it hurt like the devil. I thought I'd cracked my skull, as the voices of the boys seemed to echo in my head. But I soon saw that I'd been brought to a great, hollow chamber. Lit by guttering lamps, it smelled strongly of night soil, and hummed with a watery sound of drips and plops and ripples. I was in the sewers, I decided, deep below the buildings and the streets.

The entrance was a round, black hole. The floor was strewn with bones of all sizes, from the hollow legs of birds to massive beef bones sucked of marrow. Along the walls ran a thick shelf, and upon it sat a dozen boys dressed in rags. There was one not more than five years old, his head resting on another's shoulder. They all watched me. Thin and pale, caked with dirt, they seemed like a colony of goblins, living in darkness, dressing in human clothes they didn't understand. They wore socks for gloves, stockings for caps; some of their coats had only one sleeve, and others none at all.

One in particular put shivers of fear in my spine. Twice the size of any other, he alone had a full set of clothes, but all too small, as though he were exploding through them. His head was a troglodyte's, beetled and bumpy; his breaths went in like gusts of wind, and out like groaning bears.

"When you're dead, you're dead, Penny," said he, his voice surprisingly soft. "You don't come back."

"What do you know, Boggis?" said little Penny. Even his words were a bit twisted, as though his mouth wasn't quite right inside. "Body snatcher dug him up, dead or not." His hands had webs of skin between the fingers, and they held the coins that Worms had given me. They jingled in that webbed fist. "Had these, didn't he? Came from his grave."

The black-haired boy only shrugged. He had a torn hat that he pushed back on his head. "The Darkey will know."

With a grunt, the giant got up from the bench. He was enormous. His head would have touched the roof of the chamber if he had had a neck. But it sat squarely on his shoulders, like a bucket on a barrel. His arms were too long, his legs too short, and in his own way he was just as grotesque as dwarfed Penny. He took one lurching step, then another, and there he stopped with his great fists dangling down, his great chest heaving.

"Prove it's him," he said. "Make him talk, then we'll know. Or look and see."

"Look for yourself, why don't you, Boggis?" said Penny. "Afraid to touch him, ain't you?"

I didn't want *any* of them to touch me, Boggis least of all. But I couldn't run away, and I dared not speak. All the boys had city accents, thick as the mud of the Thames, and whoever they thought I was must have been the same. The moment I opened my mouth they would know I wasn't him.

Boggis came no closer. "We need the Darkey," he said, and turned his bucket head toward the door.

As though at his command, footsteps rang on the brick.

They grew louder and closer. Every boy in the chamber turned to watch. Even the candles seemed to brighten, nodding their flames toward the entrance.

A hope came to me—a silly, childish hope—that my father would storm through that black hole and carry me away.

I gripped my coat, the dead boy's coat, to stop my hands from shaking.

A shadow slid along the wall. It leapt around the corner and soared to the height of the chamber. It was the shadow of a humpbacked ogre. But through the entrance came only a tousle-headed boy with a stick on his shoulder and a bundle hanging from its end, resting on his back. I knew the bundle at once; it had belonged to the blind man.

The boy heaved the stick sideways from his shoulder. The bundle landed with a thump; the stick slipped from its knot and clattered on the brick among the scattered bones.

"Found this at the river," he said. "I did, or my name ain't Jack Skerritt. It was jammed in the stones at the Tower Stairs."

I knew that place, and it wasn't where I'd wrestled with the blind man. If I had fled up the Tower Stairs I would have come to the Great Tower Hill and the Tower itself, not the maze of alleys where I had met old Worms.

But as Jack knelt down to open his bundle, a sudden dread came over me. If he had found it at the Tower Stairs, then the tide must have taken it there. And if the tide had done that, had it taken the blind man too? I heard his grunts and saw, again, the spittle flying from his mouth. Had I hit him hard enough to kill him? He had been groping for his stick and bag when I'd last looked back at him. But maybe he hadn't made it far and had finally collapsed in the mud. The dark river might have carried him and his bundle away.

I would be found out. I was sure of it then. Sooner or later it would happen, and no one would believe my story. A judge would look down from a bench and ask what sort of monster would kill a helpless old blind man. There was no doubt that I would hang for what I had done.

Jack was picking at the string that tied the bundle, telling the story of his wonderful find, how he had thought at first that he had stumbled on a dead body. "Looked like a floater," he said. "But this is better. Just you wait and see."

Bending his head, he bit into the string, then stopped. "By jabers, I found these, too." He turned out his feet, looking down at them, and I saw that he was wearing my shoes. "Think of the boy what had them. A little chickabiddy boy he must have been, dancing in these fancy shoes. Wouldn't I have liked to wring his neck?"

"Didn't you, then?" asked Boggis, standing above him.

"No. They was tangled up in the bag and the stick," said Jack. "Good shoes. A touch too small, but I fixed it, see."

He turned his leg a bit farther, and I saw that he had sliced the toes open to make room for his feet. For some reason, that hurt me more than anything. After all my perils and my troubles, to see my fine shoes cut open for the big stupid feet of an urchin made a moan rise in my throat. Jack turned to look at me.

"Christmas!" he said. "Is that the Smasher?"

"Poz!" cried Penny. "Ain't you got eyes, Jack Skerritt?"

"A spirit or a person?"

The giant answered. "No one knows."

"I'll tell you soon enough." Jack looked down at his stick, then up at the lamps. "Do you think a spirit burns?"

There was one breath from all the boys. Water dripped and plopped, and the shadows moved as Jack Skerritt stood and took a lamp from the wall. The flame leapt in yellow wriggles.

"Take it, Boggis," he said, holding out the lamp. "Go on. Take it, Gaskin."

The giant's lips cracked open. His grunting breaths made the flame shiver and shrink, as though even a lamp cowered before him.

43

"Take it," whispered Jack, and the giant did. He carried it toward me, then dropped heavily at my side. "Who are you?" he grunted.

The lamp moved toward my cheek. I felt the heat of its flame; I saw its fire leap and curl.

What could I do but lie there? I wasn't a coward, but I wasn't a fighter either. I couldn't battle a giant and a roomful of boys; I couldn't even cry for help. I only watched the flame, and felt it touch hot fingers to my cheek.

But then it drew away. The same booming and splashing that had brought Jack Skerritt started anew.

"Here comes the Darkey," said Gaskin Boggis.

Six
THE DARKEY'S DECISION

Water dripped and splashed. The shadows moved. I expected the Darkey to be huge and muscled, brown as chestnuts. But none of my imaginings could have prepared me for what came through the entrance.

The Darkey was a woman. She was small, thin, as shiny as a pot of boot blacking. She came into the chamber with golden hoops in her ears, in a dress of bright colors and a hat like none I'd seen. There was a bird atop it, a full peacock, dead and stuffed, with its feathers in a bright fan. In its dozens of eyes shimmered every color of the rainbow.

"Hallo, boys," she said.

They greeted her like a mother. Most went swarming to her, and the smallest boys pressed themselves against her legs, clinging to the dress that billowed from her hips. Gaskin Boggis, though huge beside her, folded up like a little boy.

Her hands were black on their tops and pale underneath, and they passed over the heads of the boys, along their shoulders and their arms.

"Good morning, all my little ones." Her voice was deep and her words came quickly, each distinct, ringing with a laughter underneath them. Her teeth flashed in a smile.

But that faded when she saw me. Her lips drew over her teeth like dark curtains, and she scattered the boys, touching them away with white-sided hands that turned all to black as she pressed them together. Her nostrils fluttered in the broad flat of her nose.

"He smells of the grave," she said.

She came down and looked at me, and the lamplight sparkled on her hoops. Her hair was as black as the threads in my mother's veils.

"Where is it you found him?" she asked, not looking away from me.

Penny answered. "In the body snatcher's wagon. Had these in his hands."

He held out the coins old Worms had given me. The Darkey plucked them from him; she tasted the metal. "Yes," she said. "These have touched a dead boy's eyes."

If she was right, then Worms had lied to me. *"I don't touch their rings or nothing,"* he'd said. But I believed the Darkey. I believed she knew all there was to know of death and life.

Her fingers pressed my skin. They touched the part of my cheek that had been warmed by the giant's lamp. He was still holding it as the Darkey looked from me to him and somehow sensed what had happened.

"A sly one you are, Gaskin. Plucky, too." She laughed. "Playing temptations with a spirit."

"Is that what he is?" asked Boggis.

"If not now, then soon enough." Her white teeth flashed. "Benjamin Penny, you knew him best. Come and look, my darling."

He slid and shuffled through the bits of bone—now on one hand and a hip, now on his knee—scuttling in quick little movements. The peacock tilted on the Darkey's hat as she bent toward me. "He watches us. He knows what goes about him," she said. "But he doesn't talk; why not?"

Penny frowned. "It's a quiz, Darkey. He ain't quite right yet. Inside, I think."

"A long time it's been since the sisters took him in," said the woman. "You *want* him back, I know. But listen." Her earrings sparkled. "They rang the passing bell for him. Your Smasher died."

The black-haired boy leaned forward from the bench. "Darkey, why don't you look and see if—"

"I see all I need to see," she said. "In the land where I was born they talk of this. They say it sometimes happens that the dead rise from their graves, and walk and talk again. But they are cold, those walking dead, and empty in their eyes. They do not watch and listen like this one. They do not look afraid like him."

"Might be you what's scaring him," said Penny.

She laughed. The feathers quivered on the peacock, the countless eyes winking.

"If our darling has come back, we will know it," she said. "Remember how he was with his fists? If this is him he will be better tonight, for now he truly has no heart."

I shuddered at the thought of that. How could it be that a boy who had been my twin in body could be so different in his soul?

"Tonight you will see," said the Darkey. "If it isn't him, then do not bring him back."

"What do we with him, Darkey?" asked the black-haired boy.

"Let Jack decide. Let Jack do the thinking, and Boggis his bidding."

The Darkey looked once more at me, then turned her attention to Skerritt's black bundle. She sat in the shadows and laughed at the things he pulled out. There were bits of glass and bits of bone, rusted nails and lumps of coal. At the sight of each worthless thing, the Darkey laughed a little louder, and Skerritt grew a little redder in his anger. He hurled his finds around the chamber: more nails; more coal; an animal's tooth; and last of all, he pulled out the blind man's boots.

All the feathers quivered on the Darkey's hat, and her laughter tinkled through the chamber. "You've done so *well*, my darling boy."

"Bleeding battered boots!" They were tied together, and Skerritt whirled them once around his head, then sent them spinning. They thumped against the brick, and even as they tumbled to the floor half a dozen boys went running to claim them, Benjamin Penny among them.

I didn't see how it happened that Penny came out of that mob with the boots. But there were drops of fresh blood on the tops of one, and two boys remained on the floor as the others got up. One bled from an arm, and the other from a thigh, but no one paid the slightest mind. Penny came in his hurry-skurry fashion, gleaming with pleasure.

"Here, Smashy," he said. "Your feet is all blisters."

He put the boots on for me, and tied the laces tightly. I tried to smile to show my thanks, but the worried look returned to Penny's face. Either the Smasher never smiled, or my attempt looked very gruesome.

The Darkey left, and Skerritt followed, with the giant

lumbering at his heels. The other boys settled down and went to sleep on their bench of brick. But Penny stayed with me, nursing the lump on my head, fussing with my dead-boy's coat. The lamps burnt themselves out, but I never moved, and I never saw them lit again. In utter darkness, hours later, we crept from the chamber and up to the streets.

I decided that I would let Benjamin Penny lead me from the earth to the light; then I would turn and run. I would run and run as fast as I could, all the way to Camden Town.

Through a tunnel and a drain we went, then out through a grating above a putrid river. Thick and brown, reeking of waste, it oozed through a canyon of decrepit buildings. Logs and timbers propped up the walls, crisscrossing over the river. It had to be the Fleet. No other wretched river flowed through such a slum. But that meant I was close to my father. He was surely in one of the prisons along the Fleet, maybe staring out at the same tall chimneys that I could see, with their feathers of coal smoke drifting into the darkening sky.

In a mob we moved along a street unlit by any lamps, I shuffling in the blind man's boots, Benjamin Penny lurching at my side. When at last we came to a lighted doorway, I saw us reflected in a windowpane, a ragged army streaming past. I saw myself shuffling, limping, and staggering, exactly like the sort of creature I was thought to be—one of the walking dead. My boots pinched and rubbed in the wrong places, and I felt as if I were trodding on coals. I had no hope of sprinting away; I could scarcely walk, let alone run.

There were more and more lights as we passed from the slums to the haunts of the well-to-do. We came from a black filth to a glittering world of carriages and white clothes. At a broad and busy street we stopped. Lamps burned on posts, over doorways, in the windows of the shops. But their light made the darkness beyond them only deeper and more mysterious, and to see the street so patched with light and black was like looking at the hands of the Darkey.

Up and down walked women in white, their long dresses pinched at the waist, their fine hats like flower boxes balanced on their heads. In the shadows of those great hats, men strolled at the ladies' sides, at the edge of the street where horse dung lay the thickest. A corner sweeper was working madly with a straw broom, clearing his path for a woman as wide as a donkey.

In our rags and filth, we were like a group of savages at the edge of a civilized world. The boys stared; they slavered, waiting for what, I didn't know. But I saw safety and freedom among the lights and the people, and I moved to the side of our group as a carriage came by, pulled by a prancing black horse. I steeled myself to nip in behind it. But across the street—in a doorway—I saw Jack Skerritt and the giant watching me intently. I peered down the street in the other direction, and in another shadowed nook was the Darkey.

"Look," said a boy. Battered caps turned all in one direction. Hands came up, pointing from the ends of ragged sleeves. "Here comes a flashing cove."

On the opposite side of the street, a dozen doorways down, a gentleman was walking by himself. A tiny black dog on the end of a leash darted in and out between his shoes, its little legs a blur. In white trousers and black coat, the man went steadily on his way, peering in the windows that he passed.

The boys divided him up; one claimed his watch and another his purse, one his little black dog. I could feel a fever rising in their blood. Their eyes grew wide. Their teeth showed between drawn lips.

The gentleman kept coming, the dog weaving round his heels, and somehow that heat—that fever—leapt to me. It

50

was frightening to feel it, but it came as strongly as the greed that my diamond had brought, and I wanted something fierce and wild to happen. I muttered with the others, willing the man to stop on his way.

At a silversmith's he did. He entered its deep doorway, sinking into the shadows. The dog sat down beside him with its stub of a tail wagging. The gentleman clasped his hands behind his back and studied the things in the window.

A cudgel was put in my hand. I didn't see who placed it there, but only—suddenly—felt its weight. My fingers closed on the handle as though they had known it for years.

Penny whispered to me, "Go on, Smashy. Lay it on him."

"Do him, Smasher," said a boy.

I didn't hesitate. I stepped forward with an eagerness that seemed to surprise nearly everyone. "It *is* him," said a young voice. "Ain't no other."

I crossed the street. The sweeper waiting there didn't even bother sweeping. He was a gray-haired, bearded veteran of his trade, and he must have known he would get no money from me. I rapped the cudgel on my palm.

It might have been made for my hand. As though I'd used it a dozen times before, I saw myself raising it high behind the gentleman's back, then bringing it down on his head. I felt it crush his hat, and I *knew* how it would jar in my hand as it met the hardness of his skull. It was alarming, how clearly I saw it.

The man neither turned around nor heard me coming. The dog did, but it only stood up on its hind legs, eager for a pat. The gent looked down at it, then began to look toward me. I saw his eyebrows rise, wondering.

"Hello, sir," I said.

I had seen the means of my escape. I couldn't outrun the boys, and I dreaded what the Darkey had in store. My only hope was to have this man protect me, and I felt safer just being near him.

But I hadn't expected him to be frightened. As he turned fully around, a look of near terror came to his face. His mouth made a little circle, and his eyebrows arched so high that they tipped back the front of his hat. Quickly, I brought the cudgel from behind my back, thrusting it toward him. "Take this," I said.

He reeled back to the depth of the doorway, until he was pressed against the window. I stepped toward him with the cudgel, anxious that he take it.

"Help!" he cried. "Help! A thief!"

"No," I said.

He shouted even louder, with horror in his voice. He held up his hands and closed his eyes. "Oh, help me. Help!" he shouted. The little dog whimpered. Pressed back against its master's feet, it piddled on his shoes.

From all directions, men came running. I heard the clicking buzz of a Charlie's rattle, and the cries of "Thief!" rang out and spread, taken up by men and women, by cabbies and sweepers and gents. It seemed that every person on every street took up the cry against me.

"Shut up! Take this!" I told the man, shoving the cudgel at him. But it was too late. The crowd closed around me, and a cabman drove his big four-wheeler right up to the doorway. At the last moment I tried to get away. I ducked below reaching arms; I battered through a tangle of legs. But there were too many men, and they overpowered me in a moment. There were hands on my sleeves, hands on my collar. A hand found my throat and pushed me down to the street.

seven
MR. MEEL PAYS A VISIT

A man came barging through the crowd, shouting, "Move aside!" and, "Let me through!" He came with such importance that he might have been next in line to the King. "Clear a path. I'm from the parish!" he proclaimed.

He was a small but powerful figure, a bundle of muscles and sinew. He wore the long coat of a parish constable, hacked off at sleeves and tail, so that he looked both ragged and official. He pinned me on the ground. I sprawled at the feet of the gentleman, who held his little dog bundled in his arms now, the two of them quivering. Both were yapping wildly, but the gent was the louder of the two. "Thank God you came," said he. "A moment later and he would have bashed my brains in."

In a trice the constable had my hands behind my back and a rope around my wrists. Then he hauled me up and took me away, tugging with his rope as he pushed me ahead, so that I stumbled like a half-wit. The gentleman followed several paces behind, asking nervously, "Have you got a grip on him now?"

We went straight to a magistrate's court. Even then, in the dead of night, the old beak was up and about. Wrapped in a cloak of near-black wool, he sat with three old ladies and a thin man, in chairs drawn close to the tortoise stove. A little clerk with a runny nose was busy with scuttle and shovel, feeding the groaning stove lumps of coal.

They all looked up as the constable propelled me into the room. "Close the door!" they shouted together.

The thin man had his back toward me. He shifted in his chair, his arms and legs writhing like four long snakes. At his feet was a briefcase; he must have been a lawyer. "Oh, it's a boy," he said.

"A thief," said the constable. "He was accostin' this nibsome gent." He tipped his head toward the quivering gentleman, who had taken a post in the corner, holding his quivering dog.

The magistrate heaved himself from his chair. With a mighty sigh he climbed to his bench, sat again, sighed again, and said, "Bring him forward."

With a twist on the rope, the constable hauled me to the bench. Above me, the magistrate peered down through little spectacles. He set them straight on his nose. "You've been here before," he said.

"No, sir," I told him.

"No?" He turned to his clerk. "Have we not seen this urchin before?"

The clerk sniffed and wiped his nose. "Many times, m'lud."

"Indeed." The magistrate opened a ledger. He took a

quill from its ink pot and scratched on the pages. "Boy, why did you accost this gentleman?"

"I didn't, sir," I said. "I was only asking him for help."

"Good Lord!" cried the gentleman, from the back. "He was asking with a cudgel."

Round the stove, the women cackled. The thin whip of a lawyer rubbed his long fingers together.

"What did he steal from you, sir?" asked the magistrate.

"Nothing, exactly," answered the gent.

"Well, vaguely, then," said the magistrate, annoyed. "Did he take *anything*? Did he strike you?"

"No, your worship."

The gentleman suddenly sounded miserable. But my spirits began to rise. I believed in the law and its truths, and saw that I would soon be free. The magistrate frowned. He closed the ledger and returned his quill to the pot. All my troubles would have ended there and then if one of the old women hadn't leapt to her feet, shouting holy murder.

"Look at 'im!" she cried. "By cracky, look at 'im, will you." Her arm came up; a bony finger pointed at my feet. "Those boots. Those is *Arnold's* boots!"

I looked stupidly at my feet, at the blind man's boots. I didn't see right away what it meant that I wore them.

"Yes, they's Arnold's." White-haired and wrinkled, she was like a witch. Her voice seemed to set the lamplights flickering. "Ask 'im this, your lordship. Ask the boy 'ow 'e come by the boots of a murdered man."

The magistrate, the clerk, the lawyer, and the ladies all fixed me with the darkest looks. The ledger was opened again, the quill taken from the pot. "Where did you get those boots?" asked the magistrate.

"I was given them, sir," I said.

"He's lying!" shouted the woman.

"I'm *not*," I snapped back. "A boy gave them to me. I know where they came from, sir. I know they belonged to a blind man, but *I* didn't kill him. *He* tried to kill *me,* and that's the truth. He nearly drowned me in the mud, and it was only my shoelaces that saved me. I spent my shoelace money on a Chelsea bun, and . . ."

I knew I made no sense. I could see it in the astonishment on the magistrate's face. Before he could speak I started again, blundering ahead.

"Please, sir, you have to believe me," I told him. "It was another boy who was here before. The one you know, that's a different boy. He looked like me—he looked *exactly* like me, sir—but now he's dead, and people think I am him. The boys, the Darkey, they all think I'm him. That's why I've got the blind man's boots, sir, because Penny thinks I'm the Smasher. So that's why I went up to this gentleman, sir; to ask him to save me. I'm a schoolboy, sir; I've done nothing wrong. You *do* believe me, don't you, sir?"

I said all this in the most heartfelt way. There seemed no reason why the magistrate shouldn't believe me, and I was greatly pleased to see him smile.

"What a remarkable story," said he. "Clerk, have we ever heard a better one than this?"

"Never, m'lud," said the clerk with a sniff.

The magistrate picked up his quill. The feather tipped and wriggled in his hand. "The prisoner will stand trial for murder," he said.

"Oh, murder. Thank you, your lordship," said the constable. I imagined he would earn a little more for bringing in a murderer than for a mere thief. He bobbed his head, then wrenched me away.

I called out to the lawyer as the rope pulled me backward. "Help me. Please," I said, stumbling toward the door. "I can pay you for it, sir. I've got a fortune, sir. I'm rich."

He stared after me, his hands on the buckles of his briefcase. Then I passed the gentleman with the little black dog, and he put his head forward and spat on my face.

That was nearly the end for me. With my hands bound, I couldn't reach up and wipe away the spittle. I felt it dribble down my cheek, and I very nearly cried.

I was driven to prison in a two-wheeled cart, with a guard who kept plucking lice from his hair, crunching each creature between his teeth. It wasn't that, nor the spittle, nor my own misery that made me ill. It was the violent rocking of the vehicle as it bore me through the darkened streets. I had never had a stomach for motion. At the age of six I had fallen from a slow-turning carousel, and a doctor had told my mother, "The boy has an imbalance in his ears."

I thought it was a blessing when we finally stopped, until I saw the walls of Newgate Prison like a dismal fortress in the night.

More than once I had passed there with my father, and always with a shudder at the horrors that lay hidden behind those walls. I had heard the shrieks, the cries, the groans, and had always hurried along. But now the walls seemed twice as sheer and twice as high. I saw the iron door of crossed bars, and it looked as though it could open only once for me—to let me in, but never to let me out.

The gatekeeper shuffled out from his place with a lamp in his hand. "Ow, it's you again," he said. "Welcome 'ome, young master."

His keys jangled as he turned the locks and drew the bolts. The door creaked. "In you go, my lad," he said.

I passed between walls that were four feet thick. My

name was entered into the prison book, a second door was opened, and a warder led me into the depths of Newgate. It rang with the clank of iron and the shrieks of the insane. But it was even worse in daylight, when the putrid fog oozed through windows and air shafts. In the exercise yard the convicts trudged round and round. A man walked the long treadmill, his back bent as he stumbled forever uphill.

In a ward full of boys I sat in a corner. They spent hours arranged in a circle, picking each other's pockets, applauding the quickest hands. None would talk to me, which suited me fine, yet they never stopped talking *about* me. "That's the Smasher," said one.

"He went mad," said another.

"He died," said a fourth. "Them sisters tried to save him."

It was my diamond that saved *me*. It busied my mind with fancies of riches, with the mystery of how it had found its way to the river. Had a smuggler dropped it on a dark night? Had a long-ago king, or a pirate, let it fall from a chest full of jewels? Or had it lain there since the beginnings of time? Where there was one, perhaps there were others, and I dreamed myself back there, searching through the mud.

Toward the end of my third day, a turnkey arrived at the ward and called my name. "You have a visitor," he said.

He took me to a vast chamber, as quiet as a crypt, where enormous arches soared to the ceiling. In a little room at the center of it all, a man sat behind walls of glass. His back was toward me, but I saw right away who it was. The thin head, the thinner neck, belonged to the lawyer from the magistrate's court.

His briefcase lay open on a polished table. He stood up as I entered, then waved me into a chair—grandly—as though the room were his private office. "Do you remember me?" he asked.

I nodded. "Yes, sir."

"My name is Meel. Mr. Meel." He sat again, bending into the chair like a folding ruler. "I have taken an interest in you, Tom, and I'd like to help." He crossed his legs. "Will you tell me about yourself?"

"Where should I begin?" I asked.

"Tell me who you are. Tell me where you live."

He seemed surprised when I told him I was from Camden Town. But he was clearly shocked to learn how my father had been taken to debtor's prison.

"How can that be?" he said. "You told me that you owned a fortune."

"I do, sir," I said. "I was getting to that."

"Then hurry, my boy," said Mr. Meel.

Off I went again, reliving the days in my mind. I walked through the fog toward London, down to the river where the blind man was. I saw the diamond in the mud, stooped, and picked it up again.

"Surely not as big as that," said Mr. Meel, staring at my fingers as they curved around the imagined stone.

"Oh, yes, sir," I said. "It was enormous."

So were his eyes just then. "And the color? What color was it, Tom?"

"Mostly gold," I said. "It was red and yellow, but . . ."

"Like a fire burning in your hand?"

"Yes, sir," I said.

He swallowed. His fingers touched the bulge in his throat. "Where is it, Tom?" he asked.

"That's part of my story," I said. "You see, I was—"

"Well, go on," he said. "I'm a busy man. You picked up the diamond, and . . . and then what, Tom?"

Was I right to think that Mr. Meel cared more about the diamond than he did about me? Or had the wealth of my great

59

jewel, and the greed it had brought, only made me too suspicious of everyone? I went more carefully after that. I told how I had wrestled with the blind man, how I hadn't meant to kill him. "He was still alive when I ran away," I said. "I swear he was still alive. They can't hang me for that, can they, Mr. Meel?"

He shook his head quickly. "No, no. Of course not, Tom. So you hid the diamond, did you?"

We were back to that jewel.

Again and again I went doggedly on with my story. I talked about Worms and his three-legged horse, about the open grave and my dead double inside it. "This is his coat," I said, plucking at the sleeve. "Now everyone thinks I'm him. But I'm not, Mr. Meel. I'm not a thief, and I'm not a killer."

"And you're not making sense," he said impatiently. "What happened to the diamond?"

"Why do you care so much about that?" It was hard for me, a boy, to speak so boldly to a lawyer. I felt myself blush as I told him, "I think you're only after my diamond."

He drew a breath, then laughed. "Well, you don't know the first thing about law. If I'm to help you, I must see the diamond."

"Why?" I asked.

"How to put it simply? In terms you'll understand . . ." He tapped his index finger on his long nose. "Look, Tom. *If* you found a diamond, and *if* the blind man tried to take it from you, and *if* you killed the poor wretch, then no one can call it murder." He blinked. "But you'll have to produce the diamond. It's what we call evidence."

Mr. Meel stared at me for a moment. "Can't you see that, Tom? Your diamond is the key."

"Then I'm lost," I said. "I know where it is, and how to get it. But how am I to do that in prison?"

"By telling *me*," said Mr. Meel. "I will fetch the diamond for you."

I didn't know what to do. Trying to give him the proper directions would be hard enough, but trying to guess if I *should* was impossible.

"Do you think I'll run off with it?" Again he laughed. "Is that what you think?"

I was embarrassed that he'd seen right through me. I shook my head, but not convincingly.

"You foolish, foolish boy," he said. "I'll tell you something, Tom Tin; I don't believe your diamond even exists."

"Do you say that I'm lying?" I asked.

"No, not at all," he said quickly. "I believe you found *something,* but not a diamond, boy. It will turn out to be a broken bottle, a bit of shiny glass." He shrugged, and smiled. "But it doesn't matter what it is. If you *believed* it was a diamond, then that's enough to save you. That's the law, Tom Tin."

The law was as foreign to me as ancient Greek. I had no way of knowing if Mr. Meel was telling the truth. If I told him where the diamond was, he might steal it and leave me in prison. But if I kept the secret, he would go away and leave me anyway. So Mr. Meel had me in an awful fix. He had me "by the bitter end," as Father would have said.

"All right," I said. "There's a boot. A big wooden boot, and if you find that it guides you there."

"How?"

Mr. Meel suddenly burst into action. He threw open his briefcase and pulled out his papers. A pencil appeared in his hand as though from thin air, so quickly did he pluck it from a pocket. He touched the lead to his tongue.

"Yes. The boot; where is it?" he said. "Tell me, Tom. Where's the wooden boot?"

He was too eager, his face too flushed with hot blood. "Wait," I said. "Please tell me. If it's enough that I *believe* the diamond's real, why do you need to see it?"

"You doubt me?" he asked. "I come here to help, and this is what I get?" He glared across the table. "I am running out of patience, Tom. For the last time, will you tell me where the diamond is?"

eight

I STAND BEFORE A JUDGE

Mr. Meel rose to his feet. He stuffed his papers into his briefcase so angrily that they tore and bent, crumpling into yellow wads. He turned his shoulders and rapped on the window to call for the warder.

I saw his face reflected in the glass, and I didn't think I had ever seen skin quite so purple. It was the color of plums.

"You'll change your tune," he said. Despite his anger he spoke in a quiet voice, as though he knew it would scare me less if he shouted. "You'll spend your last days in the condemned cells, where the bell rings at midnight and someone prays for your soul. You'll hear the workers test your scaffold. And then, my boy, you'll change your tune. You'll shout from your cell; you'll scream through the windows for someone to help you. Down on the street they'll listen to your cries and say, 'Look at the mad boy there.' "

The warder's key turned in the lock. Mr. Meel stepped toward the door. "You've brought this on yourself, Tom Tin."

I sat at the table, shocked into silence. As I watched the warder lead him out I very nearly called him back. But then the door slammed shut, and he was gone.

Through that day and the night, every minute of every hour, I cursed Mr. Goodfellow. Everything had begun with him, and all for a debt that to him was a trifle. I imagined doing terrible things to him, things with my fists, with cudgels or knives. I imagined them so vividly that I saw his face and heard his cries.

But was I right to blame him? A whisper came from my own mind, from my soul, that I was getting just what I deserved. I had killed the blind man. I had bashed him with the diamond and let the river drown him. I had taken his life, and now mine was to be taken too. *It's only fair,* said my whispering voice. *It's only right.*

With all my mutterings and agonies, the boys in the ward pulled even farther away. I had nearly a quarter of the room to myself, but I huddled in the tiniest space, and under my breath I prayed for one more chance.

As though from Providence, it came in the morning. Mr. Meel returned to Newgate, and I met him in the same room. This time he didn't stand up. He wasted no time, but went straight to his business.

"I've just come from Camden Town," he said. "I went to the address you gave me. There was a woman there, in mourning clothes."

"My mother," I said, my hopes beginning to rise. "Was she well?"

"Well enough," said he. "I told her I had seen her son, and do you know what she said?"

"What, sir?" But then I knew, and I pressed my hands to

my temples, wishing I had thought to warn the lawyer of my mother's madness. "She told you, *'I have no son.'*"

"Not quite," said Mr. Meel. "Much the same, though, I suppose. She told me that her son was dead." He set his fist on the table. "Now you've played me for a fool and—"

"Wait!" I cried. "She's angry at me. She's half mad, you know. If you find my father, he'll tell you the truth."

"Ah, yes. Your famous father in his debtor's prison," said Mr. Meel. "I don't suppose you know which prison?"

I shook my head. "No, sir. But it must be near the Fleet."

"So I'll wander from one to the other, shall I, until I find a fellow who says 'I have no son.' And that will be your father, half mad as well?"

"He isn't mad," I said. "He's a captain."

"Then what's the name of his ship?"

I sighed. "He has no ship."

"A mother without a son, a captain without a ship. And a boy without a hope." Mr. Meel laughed. "What a sorry state of affairs."

It seemed he had come back only to torment me. In his chair he smiled. "You *are* the little monster, aren't you?" he said. "Tell me, boy. Did you feel the slightest twinge when you cut the blind man's throat?"

"I didn't," I said.

There was a look of smugness on his face.

"I mean I didn't cut his *throat.*" I put my hands on the table and leaned forward as he leaned back. "Listen, sir. I hit him, it's true. I hit him very hard; I know I did. But I didn't cut his throat, and he was still alive when I left him."

His expression never changed. "You took his boots. You wear them still."

"I was given them," I said. "I've told you that. A boy found them in the river. He must have killed the blind man."

Mr. Meel nodded. I smiled, thinking that at last I had convinced him. But instead, he sneered. "What an ingenious fellow you are."

He stood up, ready to leave. "Your trial is tomorrow. Watch the judge, boy. The judge has a black cap; it sits before him on the bench. If he puts on that cap when he delivers his sentence, it's death for you, boy." His smug smile returned. "But you'll see for yourself, and the world will be rid of you soon after. It will be the better without you, I say. Even the sewers of Fleet will be cleaner. Yes, I know your lot, the Darkey's gang."

"That's not my *lot*," I said. "It was never my lot." Mr. Meel backed away as my voice rose. "I go to school in Camden Town. Ask my teacher. Ask Mr. Goodfellow, he—"

"*Alex* Goodfellow?"

"Yes. He—"

"How could you know *him,* a fine man like that?"

"Because he sent my father to prison," I said.

A change came over Mr. Meel. I couldn't tell if he was amused or surprised, but he was different now. "Alex is in the court this very minute," he said. "I saw him not an hour ago."

"Ask him, then," I said.

"What will he say?" asked Mr. Meel. "That he knows no boy called Tom? Or that the Tom he knows is dead?"

I gasped. That was exactly what Mr. Goodfellow would say. He had seen my dead twin. He had gone into the doctor's surgery as Worms had come out. I realized then what I should have known before. It must have been Mr. Goodfellow who had told my mother I was dead.

"Bring him here," I said. It was terrible that my very last hope lay with Mr. Goodfellow, but there was no getting around it. "I'll tell you everything," I said. "If you bring him here, I'll tell you where the diamond is."

He must have sprinted all the way to the court, his brief-case flying behind him like a kite. It was not an hour later when I was brought again to the place of columns and arches. In the glass-walled room at the center, Mr. Meel was sitting in the chair behind the table. And standing in the corner was Mr. Goodfellow, as fine as ever, with the light glittering on his watch fob and chain, on the silver handle of his walking stick. His fingers were tapping on that bright, shining knob.

He looked up at the sound of footsteps. Peering through the glass—from light into darkness—he had to squint to see what lay beyond it. When I was very close he saw me, and a look of amazement came over him. There was no hiding it; he was shocked to see me. But he gathered himself quickly, and by the time the warder opened the door, Mr. Goodfellow looked more puzzled than anything.

Mr. Meel held up a hand, the palm toward me. "Don't talk," he ordered, then turned to Mr. Goodfellow. "Alex, do you know this boy?"

Mr. Goodfellow tapped his fingers on his lips. It was a nervous habit of his, I supposed, to tap them on something. He shook his head slowly. "I don't believe I do," he said.

"What?" I cried. "It's me. It's Tom Tin."

"Tin?" said Mr. Goodfellow. "Tin?" he said again, with wrinkles in his brow. "Why, the name means nothing to me."

"You're lying," I snarled. "You destroyed my father. You'll destroy us all."

Mr. Meel sprang from his chair. "Damn you, boy," he said, with bubbles of spit at his mouth. "I'll see you hang before the week is out. Jailer, take him away!"

The warder tugged at my arm. But Mr. Goodfellow said, "Please wait. Perhaps the boy has something to say that he doesn't wish for a jailer or a lawyer to hear. Perhaps I should have a word with him in privacy."

"You're too kind," said Mr. Meel. "Bless you, Alex, but you're wasting your time."

"Oh, it's only a moment, sir." There was the kindliness of a saint in his voice. "I should never forgive myself if I didn't allow that."

We were left alone in the little room as the warder and the lawyer stood beyond the glass. Mr. Goodfellow lowered his voice to a whisper. "How can this be?" he asked. "I saw you lying dead, yet here you are. It is *you,* isn't it? You are Tom Tin?"

"You know I am," I said. "Why do you deny me?"

"You left me no choice," he said. "Your father believes you're dead and gone."

"Why?" I asked.

"Because he saw you, boy," said Mr. Goodfellow. "Or your double, or whoever it was. I took him round to Dr. Kingsley's, and it fairly knocked the stuffing from him to see you lying there on the slab. But he's a strong man, and he'll pull himself together. He'll go back to the sea. It's what he wants, at any rate, to be rid of the albatross of his family."

"That's not true," I said.

"Oh, yes, it is. You've been a great disappointment to him, Tom. Selfish and spoiled as you are. He wasn't surprised that you ran away."

"I didn't," I said, blushing.

"But that's how he saw it." Mr. Goodfellow glanced toward the glass. "I need him, Tom. For this new venture of mine."

"But what about me?" I said. "They're going to hang me."

"Nonsense, Tom!" He reached out and gave my arm a little shake. "Why, they don't hang *boys.* Not anymore. Granted, you might spend some time in prison, but it will do you a world of good. Breaking stones . . . I don't know . . . whatever it is you do. It will put muscles on your arms." He pinched me there, on one thin arm. "You'll come out a man, all the better for it. Why, I shouldn't be surprised if you thank me one day."

"I'll *ruin* you," I said. "I swear to God, I will. I'll do to you what you did to my father, and ten times more."

He laughed. His cheeks bounced; his eyes teared. "That's the spirit, Tom." Then he clapped me on the shoulder and motioned for the jailer. "It will all turn out for the best, you'll see. Look for me in the court, Tom."

I did, the next day. I was taken through a tunnel and straight up to the Old Bailey, into the dock. Emerging that way, into an enormous room of chandeliers and shining wood, I felt as tiny as a cockroach. Far on the other side, the judges, in wigs and gowns, sat in a row along their curved bench. The men of the jury filled the box on my right, and down below—between the judges and me—the gentlemen of the court bustled at their work. Nearly every man held a handkerchief to his nose, or fanned himself with his hat, for the fog was thick that morning, the smell overpowering.

I was frightened, standing there. I looked down into a pit full of white wigs and black gowns, a den of lawyers. I looked up at the gallery, at the high seats half hidden by great columns, where people paid to watch the court. There, in the shadows, white in the gray, sat Mr. Goodfellow. He stared right at me, his top hat balanced like a drum on his lap, his fingers rapping on its top.

My name was called out. Men bustled around, ledgers were opened, and the lawyers' den was like a pit full of squirming snakes. The judge coughed and cleared his throat. "Who's acting for the prosecution?" he asked.

"I, my lord," answered a voice from the pit. Up to his feet rose the skinny Mr. Meel.

My jaw dropped. The one man I'd thought might help me was an agent of the other side. It was his business to send me to prison, or worse, and he set about it with a fever.

He called witnesses. One by one they mounted to the little wooden box, where a slanted mirror flashed sunlight in their faces. The gentleman who had feared being hit by my cudgel, the old woman who had shouted about Arnold's boots, the tough little constable, they all climbed up and told their parts in the story of how I had killed the blind man. Then came a fellow I had never met. He pointed at me, and told the court what a rogue and a wretch I was. He rattled off a list of deeds I had done, none of it true.

Mr. Meel bowed to the judge and took his seat. The jury was sent out, and I was marched down the steps to the holding cells. But hardly had I settled there when I was marched back up again. It had taken the jury only seven minutes to decide my fate.

"The prisoner will stand," said the judge.

I was already standing. My knees were shaking.

The judge watched me from his bench. In front of him, on a little pad, was set the black cap that Mr. Meel had told me about. *"If the judge puts on that cap . . . , it's death . . . ,"* he'd said.

The judge's fingers crept toward it now. "What does the jury say?" he asked.

High in his shadowed seat, Mr. Goodfellow drummed with his fingers.

nine
I MEET A YELLOW MAN

The men of the jury said I was guilty. "Guilty, my lord," said the foreman.

The judge reached out across his bench. His fingers touched the black cap. "Tom Tin, you have been found guilty of murder," he said. "There is no worse crime than the crime you have committed. There can be but one sentence for it."

An utter silence fell on the court. I heard the gas lamps fluttering, and the rhythmic tap-tap-tap of Mr. Goodfellow's twitching fingers. But just as Mr. Meel had said, I looked only at the black cap. It was the only thing in my world.

The judge's fingers touched it, turned it, set it straight on its little pad.

"According to the law," said the judge, "a murderer must be put to death. I have no choice, Tom Tin, but to sentence you to execution."

His fingers were slight and slender. They cupped over the round of the black cap. They lifted it from the pad.

"In light of your age, however, your sentence shall be commuted." The cap fell back to its place. The judge took up his quill and said in a slow, deep voice, "You shall be transported beyond the seas, to such place as His Majesty and His Privy Council shall direct, for the term of seven years."

"Beyond the seas!" How terrible those words sounded in my mind. The fate was the same as being hanged, to me; it was *worse* than being hanged.

I couldn't stop the groan that came to my lips. But I squeezed the railing and did not move. I stared right back at Mr. Goodfellow, though he was only a blur in my eyes. I looked at him as the men led me away, down the steps to the tunnel.

I thought I'd be taken straight to a coach, straight to a ship, and off beyond the seas. But I had one more night to spend in Newgate, and I passed it in a wretched cell, with a wretched yellow man.

He was my guard, my watcher. Gaunt as a skeleton, more yellow than London fog, he was bright as amber, a ghastly hue.

He set himself up in the farthest corner of my cell, with a candle in a holder. "Don't come near me, now," he said. "You stay over there, you hear."

The cell grew dark, but the yellow man never left his dim circle of light. He seemed delighted by my suffering.

"Beyond the seas," he said. "Good riddance, I say. It's the likes of you that done this to me. Filthy boys, you gave me the fever and the wasting disease. But I'll outlive you all." Even his laugh sounded nervous. "Hee-hee. I'll outlast the lot of you."

He lay on his side, watching me. His hair was sparse, his

skull wrinkled like a great lemon. Outside the prison, clock bells struck the passing hours.

"If not the fever, the scurvy will do you in." His fingers rubbed together like yellow pencils. "I'm dying, boy. I'm rotting from the inside out, but I wouldn't change places with you."

He coughed and muttered, twitched and groaned, as though he would die before my very eyes. The clock bells struck ten, eleven, twelve. They counted every hour, until the grimy panes of my one small window turned from black to gray. Then guards came in.

They chained me at the ankles and chained me at the waist, and marched me through the prison to a coach that waited by the door. I sat inside it, behind barred windows, and went riding out of Newgate, into the fog that was gathering again. It tumbled from rooftops and flowed over walls, and we seemed to race it through the London streets and across the Thames to Surrey.

We passed close to my old house, close to the churchyard where Kitty was buried, then swung by the river at a place I knew well.

My mother had taken me there, when I was seven or eight, to watch my father sail away in a funny-looking ship. It was as though my mother sensed that it would be his last. Before then, I had watched him go to sea only from the parlor, as he hoisted up his wooden box and went whistling from the house. I had never seen him on a ship, so this was exciting and disappointing, too. It had looked like a coster-monger's cart, old and filthy. But Father had come to the side and waved at us, and I'd waved back, shouting, "Goodbye!" as he went past very slowly, toward the Isle of Dogs.

Kitty had been with us, though she would be dead within the year. These were the last of our happiest days. I held

Kitty's hand, and she held Mother's, and we walked round the docks and past the ships. We would never go walking again. We took such a long route home that Father almost gained the house before we did. Certainly his ship had already sunk, for he'd arrived before dawn, with his trousers soaked to the knees. "It was meant to happen," he'd said. "He planned it, that . . . that *cadger!* That Mr. Goodfellow."

I hadn't known it then, but all our troubles had started that day. Mr. Goodfellow had lured my father into his company with promises of fine ships and long journeys. My father had leapt to it, seeing an end to all his years of waiting for a place in a shrunken navy, a relief from his work on the river, in the colliers and barges that never saw blue water. He had gone so happily to sea that last time, only to find that Mr. Goodfellow had given him a floating wreck. Old and rotted, it was destined to sink. Mr. Goodfellow had counted on that, insuring the ship so heavily that its loss made him one of the richest men in London. My father tried to expose him, to stand against him, but no one would listen. He went raving one day into Mr. Goodfellow's club, he in his old uniform among the powdered dandies with tight-fitting breeches and cinched waists, and the commotion he raised earned an item in the *Times*. All of London knew that my father had splashed a glass of brandy into the crimsoned face of Mr. Goodfellow. From that day onward, we had grown poorer as Mr. Goodfellow had grown richer. My father went back to his begging in the Admiralty halls, but Mr. Goodfellow's pull was stronger, and no ship ever came my father's way. We slipped into debt, and then into ruin. And now it was all for a slight—and a glass of warm brandy—that I was heading east in a coach with barred windows.

It carried me from Surrey and along the road to Chatham. It rocked and lurched on the hardened mud, and I was sick as a dog from the motion. When at last it arrived at the Medway, early in the dawn, I was glad my journey was over. I had no thought for what lay ahead. Really, my journey had only begun.

There was a mist on the river as the sun came up, nothing like the vile fog of London. White as salt, it was a cold pleasure to breathe as I clattered down a gangway to a small dock, to an open boat resting beside it. There were two oarsmen in the middle, a guard at the front, a boy at the back in chains. Though I didn't know him, he was instantly familiar. I had seen him a thousand times, in every painting ever done of farmers in their fields. Sunburned and muscled, in breeches stained by grass, he seemed as out of place in that little boat as a hayrick on the Strand. His big farming hands tugged at his chains, and tears streamed down his cheeks.

The oarsmen held on to the dock as the guard pushed me into the back of the boat. It tipped with my weight, and again with his, so that I nearly spilled over the side. He pressed me down on the backseat, then sat there himself, clutching my chains, grumbling about the fog. The oarsmen pushed us into the stream, then wrestled with their blades in a way that sent the boat sloshing from side to side. My innards sloshed with it, gurgling up toward my throat.

The current swept us away. We went swirling from the dock like a leaf in a gutter as the oarsmen fitted their oars. Gray pilings went by, with gray birds at their tops and gray buildings behind them. Then the long blades thrashed at the water, and the fog hid everything. Each pull on the oars sent the boat surging forward and me rocking back. Each push shoved the handles nearly to my chest, so I feared that any moment might find me tumbling from the back of the boat. I thought of falling through that water, my chains dragging me down, and I huddled into a little space.

The rowers kept glancing over their shoulders—at nothing at all, it seemed. But three times they pulled, then once they glanced, over and over, in such constant motion that it made me even more ill to watch.

A heavy chain appeared, then others, with no beginnings or endings to any of them. They arched through the fog like strands of gigantic cobwebs, as though their only purpose was to lash the mist in place. Then a shape formed ahead, a great wooden wall. For a foot above the water it was plastered with mussels and barnacles, with weeds that trailed in the river like eels swimming by. Plank upon plank it rose, forever, it seemed, to a top that I couldn't see. There were tiny square windows, closely barred, each fitted with a wooden lid hinged at the top. A face was at one, and it scared me to see it. A ghost could have been no whiter.

From each window came sounds of creaks and groans and coughs. From each poured a foul stench, a feeling of sadness and despair. The guard beside me covered his face with his hand, and for a moment there was pity in his eyes.

A flight of steps appeared ahead, then vanished behind, and our little boat plowed through rafts of waste, as though we floated down a sewer. We passed the back of the ship, then came to the front of another. A wooden beak jutted above me, and I stared up at the round holes of the toilets, at the wood splattered with filth. The guard mumbled through his hand. "Here she is, boys. The old *Lachesis*."

It seemed a fitting name. Lachesis was the ancient Greek Fate who measured the thread of a man's life.

"No place like home," said the guard.

ten
MY ARRIVAL ON THE HULK

In the shadow of the terrible ship, the farm boy moaned. "No!" he cried. "God spare me!" And he began to struggle.

He thrashed in his seat, pulling at his chains. The guard held him down, and in the struggle the boat rolled nearly to its side. One of the rowers swore at him to sit still. But the farm boy struggled harder, tipping the boat so far that water came pouring over the side. Then the guard bashed with his fists, and the rower turned in his place to help him, and the farm boy toppled face-first into the bottom of the boat. There, curled on his side, he lay weeping in the puddled water until we bumped against the side of the ship.

The guard hauled him out and dragged him up the steps. "No! Please, oh please," cried the farm boy as he went sobbing into the mist.

I hobbled after him, clanking in my irons. I stepped onto

the ship, over a brown bundle that lay right in my path, a bulge of cloth like a big cocoon. Three jailers waited there, all in uniform. The guard gave them a packet of papers that he drew from his jacket, then stripped away our irons and hurried down the stairs. For the first time since leaving Newgate I put my feet together and raised my hands as high as my shoulders. But I felt no pleasure doing it.

In the white silence of the fog, the ship was a black and shabby ruin. How it would carry me across the seas I couldn't possibly imagine. It had only stumps for masts, a few tarry strings of rigging. At the front it was built up into a shadowy slum of tilted shacks. At the back was a higher level, where wicked-looking cannons aimed their mouths toward me. Up there, a bell rang. Another, in the distance, tolled at almost the same moment.

As though the ship had been wakened by the bell, a sound swelled up from below, a steady drumming and a ringing of metal that made the very timbers shake. Then through the hatches came the convicts. By the dozen, by the score, they tramped in long, straight lines. All were silent, hunched, weighted down with chains. They were boys every one, boys of every size, boys of every age. They moved in a sound of shuffling feet and scraping metal, each carrying a brown bundle, a smaller and neater version of the one that lay by the steps.

Guards shouted at them to "Move along!" and "Hurry now!" They beat the boys with ropes, with canes, but the boys never cried out. The lines stretched from the hatches to the wooden shacks. Each boy went in with his bundle and emerged without it, and shuffled again to the hatches. Over the sills, into the ship, they went like brown ants to their holes.

A man with a shovel worked his way between the lines. He paused at the steps to hoist the bundle that lay there onto his shoulders, and the cloth fell open as he lifted it. A bony arm came out, the fingers drooping, and I glimpsed a pale shoulder, a thatch of dark hair—a dead boy, wrapped in canvas.

When the deck was empty, the jailers dragged us along. They took our clothes away and hosed us down in the bitter spray of a pump. The water blasted at my head, at my feet, at my spine and ribs as I twirled on the deck, flinching at the icy shock, ashamed of my nakedness. The farm boy lowered his face. His hands cupped over his privates, his eyes closed, he stood as still as a rock while the water sprayed from his chest in rainbows. Men scrubbed our skin with long-handled brushes that seemed to have nails for bristles.

We were given prison clothes of the drabbest brown, patched at elbows and knees. My trousers were so big that I begged for a bit of rope to hold them up. We were given tin bowls, tin spoons, and two old rags—one a handkerchief and the other a cap. Then out from the shacks came a blacksmith, a great black man dragging chains from his hands. The farm boy dropped to his knees.

"Please!" he cried. "Don't chain me again." He clasped his hands together and held them above his bowed head as though in prayer. "I won't run away. I swear it."

A guard hit him on the shoulders with a rope end. Another used a cane, and they knocked the boy flat on the deck. In a moment the irons were on him—a chain at each leg, a chain at his waist—and the guards laughed to see him writhe on the deck like a half-stunned fish.

It was awful to see him so humbled, so small, and I put up no struggle when my turn came. But the chains jingled—link to link—as I stood and quivered there. Twelve pounds I bore on each ankle, more at my waist. It seemed like a ton of metal.

When I saw a man bearing down the deck in a uniform with shining buttons, I was sure he was coming to set me free. He would say that a mistake had been made. "A terrible mistake," he would say.

Short and stout, round as a juggling peg, he looked the picture of self-importance. He must have come straight from his breakfast, as a blot of mustard perched on his lip like a yellow boil. It was all I could look at when he stopped in front of us.

"I'm the Overseer," he said. "This ship is mine. *You* are mine. Is that clear?"

"Yes, sir," I said. The farm boy merely nodded.

"There are only two rules on my ship." He spoke slowly, stretching his words. "Two rooools," he said. "Behave yourselves; that's one. And don't make trouble; that's the other."

They seemed one and the same to me, but I didn't point it out. My hope had faded already.

The Overseer's eyes were as hard as stones. "If you behave yourselves, you'll find me very lenient." *Leeeenient,* he said. "I might strike off one of those irons; I might strike off the other. I might grant you little liberties."

He licked his lips, and the mustard disappeared.

"But make trouble, and trouble awaits. Those irons will be doubled; they'll be trebled. You'll feel the cane on your back and find the black hole waiting. How you pass your time aboard my ship is up to you. Is that clear?"

"Yes, sir," I said.

"I keep two lists." He held up two fingers, as though to help us count. "The first is for transportation. If you're on that list, you're bound for Van Diemen's shore, off beyond the seas, perhaps never to return. Is that clear?"

"Yes, sir." That was the only fate I'd expected.

"The other list recommends boys for liberty. Behave well, improve yourselves, and freedom awaits." He winked—or twitched; I couldn't be certain. "Now, the only way you'll leave my ship is to be put on one of those lists. You work aboard and sleep aboard; you never go ashore. If you're not pardoned, if you're not transported, you'll spend every year, every hour of your sentence within these wooden walls. Is that clear?"

"Yes, sir," I said again.

He held out his hand for the packets of paper, then shuffled through them. "Tom Tin," he said, "you've been found guilty of murder and sentenced to seven years transportation. Oten Acres, to the same for the theft of a sheep. You'll find seven years is a very long time if you spend it on the *Lachesis*. But I'll tell you, boys; either of you could find yourselves on my list in less than six months."

"On which list, sir?" I asked.

His face darkened. The gray eyes turned to black. "Did I ask you a question?" he said.

"But, sir, I—"

His hand shot out and slapped my face. "Silence! You speak only when you're told. Guards, take them below."

He turned his back as we were hauled away. The guards pulled and pushed us to the hatch, where stairs went steeply into darkness. A foul, hot air wafted up, the breath and the sweat of five hundred boys. I heard them down there, in a banging and a ringing that I didn't understand and didn't wish to know. A single cry echoed through the space, a moan of wretched suffering. Into my mind came the voice of my teacher, reading in his deep voice—from a red leather book—the words Dante had found at the gates of hell: "All hope abandon, ye who enter here."

"Down you go," said the jailer.

I stood for a moment, not looking into the hole, but at everything else. The fog was thinning, and I could see the whole ship, from the shacks and animal pens to the big ensign hanging limp at the back. On one side of the river was a stretch of mud and marsh; on the other a grim old castle. The *Lachesis* sat not quite in the middle, anchored in a row with two other hulks. High in the water, ungainly and ugly, they were chained at their moorings, as though if left to themselves they might flee. There was a forest at the northern bend, the dockyards at the south.

I wanted to remember it all—the way the water was dazzled by the silver light, how the forest was a smudge of green and brown, the way the redbrick buildings of the dockyard huddled in a pall of smoke.

"Down!" said the jailer. He whacked my shoulders with a knotted rope.

The farm boy cried out again. He braced his feet on the hatch, then grabbed at its edge. I saw his eyes—huge with terror—as the guards wrestled him below.

There was nothing that could save me, no one who could help. In one hand I held my chains, in the other my bowl and spoon, and I knew it was all I would own for the next seven years. Down into the ship I went, down to a deck and down to another. I sank into that thing body and soul, and the very air thickened with sweat and lamp oil and filth, until I could *see* it swirling before me. At the lowest deck I could only barely stand upright. The guards had to bend their heads, and big Oten Acres slumped in a slouch, with his neck turtled into his shoulders.

Since the morning I had left home, I had been like a football, kicked from place to place, from person to person, rolling all the time downhill. Now I could go no deeper without sinking through the river and into the earth itself. To get out again I would have to haul myself up. And I decided right then that I would not spend even six months on that ship.

Massive timbers arched from the walls and crossed the ceiling from side to side. Little grated windows let in such small light that lamps flickered everywhere, and all was brown and dismal. Amid the frame of wooden bones, as though in the belly of a whale, the boys of the hulk were at breakfast. On benches, at tables, they sat in silence before bowls of food. All were as pale and bony thin as the body that had been bundled on the deck. It seemed that rows and rows of skulls were staring from the darkness.

A man said, "Boys! The blessing," and up they stood. Their irons made a single clang, their canvas clothes a single rustle. All at once, and all together, they lifted their bowls and chanted their thanks to God.

Then they sat again, and a moment passed. I heard a creak in the ship's wood, and felt the hull shift below my feet. I lurched sideways, dizzied by a movement that I could feel but not see.

"Begin," said the man.

It was as though he had started a race. Spoons came up from the tables. Heads went forward, elbows out. Animals at a zoo couldn't have eaten more ferociously. Each boy guarded his bowl from the others, and the only sound was the clink of tin on tin, from hundreds of spoons in hundreds of bowls, a rattle that I would never forget if I lived a thousand years.

I was pushed to a place at the foot of a bench, and Oten was pushed to the opposite one. A dozen boys sat shoveling food from bowl to mouth, and another only stared at us from the head of the table. He was just as pale as the rest, but not so gaunt or sickly-looking. His bowl was heaped while the others were half full, and I guessed that he was the leader, a sort of king in a little kingdom of wasted boys. It was impossible not to stare back. A scar ran clear across his face, from cheek to cheek, like a white rope buried in his skin. It split his nostrils and curled his lip, then ran in jagged bursts nearly to his ears. Above it, his eyes shone like a rat's, and I felt there was nothing behind them but the cunning of a rat—no sadness or joy, no thoughts for a single thing other than staying alive.

"A pretty picture, ain't I?" he said.

83

I turned away, nearly bumping into a boy who stood at my elbow. He held a bucket—a wooden bucket full of breakfast—and a ladle that dripped the slop into my bowl, and into Oten's next. Nothing I had ever seen had looked so gray and awful. When I put my spoon into the blobs and curdles, a weevil came bubbling up.

I had gone almost a full day without food, but I couldn't eat *that*. Even old Worms with his scavenged bones would have left it lying by the roadside. As I looked down in disgust, the hulk groaned around me. A lamp hanging from the timbers began to turn and sway. The slop shifted in my bowl, and the weevil tipped on its side.

My stomach was a bubbling pudding, my brain a swirl of fog. The ship seemed to be moving. The shadows from the lamps slid up and down the timbers. At the end of the table the scarred boy said, "I remember you."

My mouth was dry as dust, my skin clammy. I didn't care about the boy or anything else. I wanted only for the motion to stop.

"The Smasher, they called you."

So my dead twin had followed me to the hulk, but I scarcely cared about even *that*. "My name's Tom Tin," I said. "I've never seen you before."

"You look like the Smasher."

I shrugged; there was nothing I could say.

"And you *sound* like him."

That was a surprise. It shocked me, for a moment, right out of my sickness. So my twin hadn't come from London after all. If his accent had been the same as mine, he must have been born within miles of my home.

"It was you what gave me this." The boy touched his scar, and it twitched into a terrible grin. "Well, things is different here, ain't they? Who's got his mates around him now?"

eleven
A LITTLE KING IN A LITTLE KINGDOM

I felt utterly miserable, woozy and hot. But even through my daze I was afraid of the boy with the scar. The others had been withered by the hulk, but he had been hardened, like a bit of steel in a fiery forge. If he thought I was someone else, how could I prove that I wasn't?

"Lads," he said. The eating stopped. Faces looked up. "This here's the Smasher, he calls himself. He'll think he's a nob, but he ain't. He's worse than a nosey, you hear."

I didn't know what he was talking about.

"Pay up, nosey." He tapped his spoon on the rim of his bowl. "You too, bumpkin boy. You both owe me a share."

I would have given mine gladly if I could. But it seemed too huge an effort to lift my bowl. I groaned to myself.

"He's got the fever," said a redheaded boy.

"Ain't the fever, Carrots," cried another. "He's seasick!"

It was true. I, the son of a captain, the descendant of fishermen, was seasick in an anchored ship in a river.

"He is! He's seasick." A laugh spread up the table and across to the next. On the whole dark deck the boys leaned left and right and stared toward me, those skeletal boys with skulls for faces. They might not have smiled in months, but now they sat in their brown clothes, in their irons, and shook with mirth. "Seasick! Seasick!" they cried. Even the guards laughed, and I doubted if that horrible ship had ever heard the laughs of boys and guards together. But it didn't last long. The guards recovered first, then beat the laughter from the boys. Heads went down again, spoons to bowls again, and the ship seemed to shrink into misery and darkness.

The scarred boy tapped his bowl again. "Pay up. Give us a share."

Oten Acres stared back with a wondering look. "Why? It's the little fellows here who need it. Like him." He pointed at the boy beside me, so small that his feet didn't touch the floor. "It's you should share with him. Big lump like you."

That little boy gasped. He wasn't more than ten years old; he couldn't have been even that. His face was still like a baby's, his hands just tiny things. "Do what he says," he whispered. "That's Walter Weedle. He's a nob."

Weedle's little rat's eyes fixed on Oten Acres. "It's share and share alike here, ain't it, lads?" he said. "You share and I like you. Don't, and you get a bruising."

"I don't want no trouble," said the farm boy. "But you've got a lot, and I've got very little."

"You've got little *sense*," said Weedle. "Now pay up, noseys."

"Please give it to him," whispered the boy beside me. "You give him yours, I'll give you some of mine."

"I don't want *any* of it," I said. "He can have the whole

see? Match 'em right, and all'sh Bob, Tom. Now look." He sewed them together. That was all there was to it, but Midgely showed me every step and every stitch. "It's easy when you get the hang of it," he said. "Now try it, Tom."

I threaded my needle and sewed my cloth together. Midgely smiled up at me with his baby cheeks. "That'sh good," he said, in his watery voice. "Oh, that'sh grand, Tom."

There were small, square windows along the wall that let in shafts of light and cold breaths of air. But still the lamps were burning, and my sickness only grew worse. It came in bursts, with each shift of the light, or every time a reel of thread suddenly rolled itself along the table. I tried to put my mind on the work, but it was the most mindless business anyone could have dreamed of, and I soon saw that it would never end. When we got near the end of the piles, more cloth appeared.

The bell tolled once.

I recited Virgil to myself in Latin, and Pliny in Greek. I made myself dizzy with Euclidean elements, and I kept listening for the ring of the bell. When my pile of doubled pieces grew, Walter Weedle reached out and took a few to add to his own, so that it seemed he did twice the work of me. The guard, each time he passed, saw my little pile and bashed me on the shoulders. "Work harder," he said. "Work faster."

We were supposed to do it without talking, but a murmur of whispers hummed in the room, and bubbles of silence followed the guards. I was reminded of frogs in a pond. But Midgely knew when to whisper and when to be silent. He asked where I was born, and why I was on the hulks. "Can you read?" he whispered. "Can you do numbers?" But I barely answered, too ill to care. Hundreds and hundreds of times I pushed the needle through the cloth and pulled it out the other side. Soon my fingertips were punctured, and drips of blood marked every second stitch.

A boy fell asleep and was bashed awake. Two others were taken from their places and marched from the room.

"They're going to punishment," whispered Midgely. "Every morning there's punishment."

"Worse than *this*?" I asked, and he laughed.

"You'll see."

They came back hunched and hobbling, their faces drawn. It seemed they had aged into old men with trembling hands.

The bell took forever to count up to eight. But finally it did, and we put aside our cloth and thread. We trooped downstairs for our dinner—a bowl of the same gray gruel, and a little chunk of waxy cheese. We held it up and chanted a blessing, and Weedle demanded his share. But Oten Acres wouldn't give up a morsel. "Get stuffed," he said, staring glumly at his food.

I remembered my father telling me once about bullies. "They're only seventh-raters, dressed up like ships of the line," he'd said when I'd come home in tears one day. "Run out your guns, Tom, and they'll strike their colors."

The only color Weedle struck was a deep and furious red. He muttered the most bloodcurdling oaths, then demanded a double share from me. I gave it up without a care, and passed the rest to Midgely. "Don't think I'm done with *you*," said Weedle.

Already I hated the bell. It rang once to start our meal, twice to end it, and we formed our lines and climbed through the ship. I followed a rut that irons had grooved in the planks, up past the workrooms and out to the open air.

I thought then that I would see the sun going down, that my first day was over. But it was only noon, not evening, and I realized that the bells counted *half* hours. With seven years ahead of me, the difference was nothing. A blink, an instant, was all it was. But the disappointment was nearly enough to break me. I lowered my head and trudged in the line, round and round the deck. My heart felt as heavy as my irons.

Seven years, I thought. I couldn't last that long. Why, I couldn't last the six *months* the Overseer had hinted at. If Weedle didn't kill me, I would die from sickness, or wither away from the sheer misery of the place. I dragged my feet until Midgely bumped up on my heels. I whispered back at him. "Do people escape? Has anyone *ever* got off?"

His child's fist pushed me forward. "Don't talk to me, Tom."

"Tell me," I said. "Yes or no."

A guard came running. He bashed me with his cane, then bashed Midgely, too. I cowered from him, ducking my head, and in the angle below his raised arm I saw the Overseer watching. I took a blow on my elbow, another on my wrist, but poor Midgely caught it worse. The cane whistled up and down, and a pathetic squeal came from Midgely's lips. But he didn't move to protect himself. He only winced and shook with each blow.

We circled the deck once more, then filed through the hatches and down to the workroom. I took my place and started sewing again. Across the table sat Oten, weeping silently. I could see the tears coming from his eyes, his tongue licking them away as they trickled down. Beside me, Midgely sewed his bits of cloth and watched the guards go back and forth.

Suddenly he leaned toward me. "People have done it," he whispered.

I didn't know what he was saying at first.

"They've escaped," he said.

twelve
THE CRIMES OF WALTER WEEDLE

I thought Midgely was clear off his nut. I couldn't believe I'd heard him properly.

"It's true," he said. "That's how they escape."

"They *tunnel*?" I asked.

"Yes, Tom. Through the planks. Through the hull."

Midgely bent quickly to his work as a guard came by. He waited, then whispered again. "The ship's half rotten. The wood's like mud in places, Tom. Look where there'sh water."

It was some sly sort of clue, I thought. Where *wasn't* there water, round a ship in a river? But a guard chose that moment to settle by our table, with his buttocks bulged against it, and we talked no more until the day was done.

The guards took our needles and thread. We went down to a dinner of boiled ox cheeks, a most disgusting sight. I watched the strands of cheese-colored fat curl over themselves like wriggling worms, and pushed my bowl away. Weedle took his share, and more, and Midgely got the rest. Across the table, Oten Acres neither shared nor ate, but only sat staring glumly at his bowl.

After dinner we trudged again around the deck, in the same weary silence. The air did me good, and I lifted my head to study the shore, thinking how I might get away. There were fishing boats in the river, and a fleet of scows and barges. In the navy yard to the south, a forest of masts grew from the wharfs and warehouses. The castle was in shadows, with the sun setting now behind it, but the marshes shone like a field of gold. There were acres and acres of grass, without a single building in sight. That was the way I would go; into the marshes and over the fields.

I went back into the ship feeling not quite so hopeless. Even my sickness was easing, and I was rather proud to think that I was finding my sea legs. We settled for the night on the lowest deck, crowded like cattle in a pen. Oten Acres lay huddled by a tiny window, staring out at the river. I was sitting with Midgely when a line of boys went marching past.

"Where are they going?" I asked.

"To chapel," said he.

"Shouldn't we go with them?" I asked.

He sneered. "Only noseys go to chapel, Tom."

We leaned against the planks, free now to talk as we wanted. In the middle of the floor, a group of boys played pitch-button with knots of thread and cloth. "Knuckle down fair!" cried one, as he might have at any playground.

"Tom?" said Midge. He touched my arm and surprised me with his question. "Do you think heaven's a hulk. Do you?"

"A hulk?" I said.

He nodded. "God's got 'em, you know. I seen 'em, Tom."

I told him I didn't know what he was talking about. So up

he got and went off to the side of the ship, and came back with a book—with two—held in his arms, at his chest. He put them down, then spread one open on the floor. "I nicked these from the chaplain," he said, turning backward through the pages, past pictures of Elijah's flaming chariot, Daniel in the lions' den, Joseph and his coat of colors. He stopped at Noah's ark and said, "There! See?"

The ark was tossed by a tempest. Round and dark, with a shack on its deck and a stump for its mast, it did look like a hulk. Faces of animals stared from round windows. The sons of Noah huddled by the cabin, fearful of the storm. But Noah himself stood up in the wind and the lightning with his long beard and white hair as wild as the spray on the water.

"See?" Midgely pressed his finger on the page. "That's God there, ain't it, Tom?"

I shook my head. "It's Noah."

"No a what?" he asked.

I thought he was joking, but he wasn't. He had never heard of Noah, or the flood that had drowned a wicked earth. He thought that the man in the picture had to be God just because he was so wild and so frightening. "There's other puzzles here," he said. He showed me Moses in the rushes, Bartimeus being cured of his blindness. I had to explain them all, astonished that he'd never learned the Bible. Then he showed me one more picture. He said, "Look, Tom. It'sh me."

He'd turned to David and Goliath. The giant was twice the height of the horses and their riders. His boots alone were taller than David. But the boy stood before him, swinging his slingshot, as though he had no fear.

"That's me," said Midge. "Me all the time. I'm always fighting giants."

He looked around before he whispered. "Weedle, he's the worst of them. He's the head of the nobs."

At the far side of the ship, Weedle was sprawled below another window. He took up three times the space of anyone else, and again made me think of a king. His courtiers were sickly and wan, but they hovered around as he lay like a Roman in his squalid splendor.

"Why is he here?" I asked.

" 'Cause he's a convict, Tom."

"But what did he do?"

Midgely moved closer. "No one knows but me," he said. "I was in court when the judge sent him here. I heard what he did."

"What?" I asked.

"You have to promise not to tell. Promise, Tom. He'll kill me if he knows I did him out."

I thought it must have been something dreadful, something beyond my imagining. I gave my promise, and Midgely whispered in my ear. "He's a snow dropper, Tom."

"What's that?" I asked.

"Why, he was smugging snow, of course. From off the hedges, Tom."

"But what's snow?"

"Shhh!" There were boys on each side of us, boys all around. They coughed with fever and moaned with dismay, and not one cared enough to listen to us. "Washing, Tom," said Midge. "The white things put up to dry. You know, Tom." His voice became even softer. "*Ladies'* things."

"Petticoats?" I said. Midgely nodded quickly, with a smile on his face, and I laughed out loud. "That's why he's here? For stealing *petticoats*?"

"Shhh!" said Midgely sharply. "He'll kill me, Tom. He really will."

But Weedle was laughing with Carrots, the long scar splitting his face so that his jaw seemed enormous. I could easily picture him prowling through the tiny gardens in the slums, plucking petticoats from hedges, and my fear of him dwindled somewhat. He was only a bully after all, full of nothing but bluster, as my father had said, the fancier of women's clothes.

"I shouldn't have told you," said Midgely. "I should have minded my tongue." He closed his Bible book. His hands worried the edges of it. "You won't say nothing, will you?"

"No," I said.

He looked worried, though. He opened the book again, then quickly closed it. "In that picture, Tom, that battle? Does the giant kill the boy?"

"No," I said. "David slayed Goliath."

"Oh, he must have been brave," said Midge. "He must have been like Acres there." Only his eyes moved toward the farm boy. "David would have said the same as him. 'Get shtuffed,' he would have told that giant."

Midge moved right beside me, his shoulder on my arm. "Don't you wish you was like that? Brave as him? If you ain't brave, you're done for here."

His words stung like slaps. I didn't think of myself as a coward, but Midgely clearly did.

"We're just bum-suckers," he said. "Me and you."

I felt myself blush. "It's not that, Midge." I told him what the Bible said, that the meek will inherit the earth. But he only frowned again and asked, "What's the meek, Tom?"

"The mild. The gentle people."

"You mean the ones what don't fight back?"

"I suppose so," I said. I didn't really know. "The Bible says not to fight your enemy. It says to turn away if he hits you, and not to cry out if he hurts you. Never hit back. Never cry out."

Midgely nodded. "That's me, all right. That's you too, ain't it, Tom?" He looked up at me, and a smile lifted his lips for a moment. "We'll inherit the earth," he whispered. "Think of that, Tom."

He put down his Bible book and took up the other. "Now read me some of this one, Tom," he said.

It was the story of a missionary who had been to the South Sea islands. The pages had been turned so often that they were torn and grubby, smeared with dirt. Midgely knew exactly where to turn to find the picture that he wanted.

"Look," he said, showing me an etching of an island. "Look at the trees. There's birds in the trees."

I couldn't see them until he pointed right at them. Tiny and blotted, they looked at first like mistakes, as though the printer's ink had dropped on the etching. But I saw the shapes repeating, the trees just full of birds.

"There'sh bonesh and thingsh." He was slurring his words in excitement. "There'sh sheashellsh on the shand," he said.

He showed me a path leading up from the beach, the corner of a house that was otherwise hidden in the forest. He showed me a fish in the water, and the fin of a shark going by. "What does it say?" he asked.

I read to him what was written underneath. "The home of the chief was a thatched hut all but invisible from the sea."

"All but invisible," whispered Midgely.

There were a lot of pictures, and he knew them all in the same detail. In each he pointed out a thing so small that I just couldn't see it, no matter how I squinted or turned the book in my hands. I never saw the spear propped against a tree, nor the face of a savage in the bushes, nor the lizard sunning on a rock. Perhaps they weren't even there. In his mind, I thought, Midgely wandered through those pictures. In the evenings, and the nights, he lived on those faraway islands.

A boy beside us leaned across to see the book. Midge shoved him away; he knocked him aside with a sharp blow that came in perfect time with the ring of the ship's bell. Decks above us, that thing started tolling. The last time it had rung three times, but now it kept going—eight strokes in all. "Someone's forgotten the count," I said.

Midgely frowned, then laughed. "We're in the dog watches," he said. "Don't you know that, Tom? You, what can read and all?"

Pleased to know more than I, he launched into a dizzying talk on watches and bells and dogs, and I *still* didn't understand. "How do you know that?" I asked.

"I grew up in the dockyards, didn't I?" he said, getting to his feet. "All I ever knew was ships and sailors."

Once more we went on deck, but only for a moment. In a long line, we threaded up the hatch and straight to the tumbling shacks at the front. The boys ahead fetched the bundles that I'd watched them bring out in the morning, going at the same plodding pace that took them anywhere and everywhere. I saw Oten Acres shuffle through the door and stop there, bewildered. A guard gave him a clout and a push; "Take your hammock," he shouted. Poor Oten doubled over. "No one never gave me one!" he cried.

Fearing the same thing for myself, I waddled through the door with my hands held out, calling, "Please, sir, I haven't a hammock!" I avoided the beating Oten had got, and thought myself lucky for that.

We tramped down to that dark lowest deck, where boys were already hanging their hammocks from the great timbers on the ceiling. "I want to be by the window," I told Midgely.

"Ain't a *win-dow*," he said scornfully. "And it ain't really a scuttle, so don't call it that." As if I ever would have. "It's a grating, Tom. All them holes, they're just carved out. 'Cept for the ones on the gundeck, where the cannons was. And anyway," he said, "there ain't a chance that you'll be sleeping there."

"Why not?" I asked.

" 'Cause you ain't a nob."

I ended up somewhere in the middle, between the noseys and the nobs, in such a crowd of hammocks that they nearly made a solid floor of canvas above the wooden one. We all stood there, our heads above the brown mass, like moles peering from the earth. A guard said, "Up!" and in a great rattle we climbed aboard the things. With twenty-four pounds of iron on my ankles, I didn't think I could do it. But I watched Midgely, then did as he did, swinging up and into a contraption that closed around me like a pod round a pea. I swayed from side to side, bumping first against Midge, then against the boy on my other side. He swore and pushed me away, so that I swayed all the harder, and hit him again.

My sickness returned, suddenly and wholly, as I gripped the sides of the hammock. At last it stopped moving, and I lay there, packed among the other boys as tightly as bats in a cave.

The lamps went out. I heard the guards tramping up the ladders, then the rattle of chains and locks.

"What's going on?" I whispered.

"They're locking us down," said Midge. "The guards never stay down here at night."

I raised my head and stared across a sea of hammocks. A murmur of voices spread through the deck. Boys coughed and muttered; some began to snore. But others cried in muffled sobs, in whimpers and sniffs. They tossed and turned in a clangor of metal.

I heard a soft thud nearby, another farther off. Metal scraped on wood as someone crawled below the hammocks. The sea of canvas, now disturbed, moved in ripples here and there.

"Don't look," whispered Midgely. "It's the nobs, Tom. At night they own the ship."

thirteen

A STRANGE AND SILENT FIGURE

From the darkness of the ship came a sudden cry of pain. High and shrill, it jolted through me, setting my nerves tingling, my heart racing.

"Lie still, Tom," whispered Midgely. His fingers were hooked on the edge of his hammock, but all the rest of him was hidden inside it. "Don't even move," he said.

The cry came again, then a thump and a scuttling sound. My mind turned the noises into visions: a boy curled on the floor with his hands on his face; feet kicking; fists pummeling.

"Ain't nothing you can do," said Midge in his whisper. "It ain't you they're after, Tom. Lie still and wait."

Wait for *what?* I wondered. No, it wasn't me they were after. Not *that* night, at least, or not that hour. But my turn would come; I knew it. "Midge," I said. I reached across and shook his hammock. "Show me where the hull is rotten."

"Now?" he said.

I didn't wait another moment. I slid from my hammock and crouched on the floor. The faintest of light came in through the grates, making gray of the black space between the floor and the bulging hammocks. With a soft tinkle of his irons, Midgely came down beside me. We crawled below the sleeping boys, along the deck to a distant grating. The light of the stars shining up from the water glowed dimly on Midge's face. He touched the wood at the base of the wall, then rapped with his fist. He did the same at the next grating, and the one after, before he looked at me and said, "Here. Look at the spirketing, Tom."

"The what?"

He took my hand and put it on a thick plank just above the deck. Even in this faint light I could see a patch of wood darker than the rest. "Tap it," Midgely said. The patch was soft and spongy.

"That's rot," he said. "There ain't enough of it here, but that's what it's like. Smell it, Tom."

I put my nose close to the wood. The smell was rich and earthy, like mushrooms in a cellar. It tickled my nostrils.

"That's what you want," said Midge.

We went right through the ship, up and down the ladders. Once we heard the boyish voices of the nobs, and once the march of heavy footsteps. As they came toward us, Midgely pressed me into the shadows behind a ladder. On the deck above, a guard went by in a circle of light from the lantern he carried. It made huge sweeping shadows of his legs.

"You said they didn't come down at night," I whispered when the guard had wandered by.

"I said they don't *stay*," said Midge. "They come on their rounds sometimes."

We held our irons tightly so they wouldn't rasp against

the wood, and went up and down, back and forth, until I was hopelessly lost. Then somehow, in the darkness, we parted. I suddenly found myself alone, with no idea where I was. "Midge!" I called, as loudly as I dared. "Midgely!" But there was no answer.

I crept through the ship. Every post and pillar, every window looked the same. I thought I was going in circles, until I found a doorway that took me to a new and different room. Benches stood in perfect rows, in a place that towered twice or thrice the height of any other deck. In a hatch far above me, the stars of the Pleiades shone in their square.

It was such a quiet and peaceful place that I could hear the river rippling against the planks. Then timbers creaked, and the ship turned a bit in the current. The moon—a curved sliver—seemed to balance on the edge of the hatch. It sent a beam of light down through the darkness, through swirls of dust, onto the face of a bearded man.

He stood in the shadows below the ceiling, many feet above the floor. Utterly still, and utterly silent, he seemed to be staring right at me.

I eased myself toward the wall, into the corner by the last of the benches. Hidden there, I waited, willing him to go. I heard the bell very far in the distance, and waited till it rang again. But the man never moved.

From somewhere in the ship came another sudden cry, and the sounds of a struggle. There was such misery in the voice that I clamped my hands to my ears. It was Midgely, I thought. The nobs had caught Midge because I had dragged him from his hammock. They'd caught Midge, and next they'd catch me.

The hull creaked and shifted, and the moon seemed to turn in the hatch. Its light, for a moment, shone more fully on the man's face, and I saw there a look of worry, of *care,* perhaps. Then the moonlight shifted away from him, across the room, and directly onto me. Too late, I dropped behind the bench. But I heard no shout, no movement. The man must have seen me, yet he stood still and quiet. I wondered if he was hiding too, tucked as he was into the top of this high, empty space. I whispered into the moonlight, "Who are you?"

His silence was unnerving. To think I shared this secret place with such a mysterious person put prickles in my skin. Yet I felt only comfort to have him there; I knew that he meant no harm to me. I could have stayed quite happily all through the night, free from worries of Weedle and the nobs. That was the sense he gave me.

But I was worried for Midgely. It annoyed me that I was, for I had never fretted about the welfare of others. What Mr. Goodfellow had told me once was true: I *was* selfish, and I knew it. I owed nothing to Midgely, so why did I want to find him?

I took off my shirt, thinking I could wrap it around my chains and muffle their sounds. I leaned against the wall, drew up my legs to grasp the irons—and there I stopped. The smell of rot was all around me, strong as smelling salts.

Everywhere on the ship, the wall was made of planks. But here it was paneled in sheets of oak that might have belonged in a rich man's home. Each square was set in its own frame, and each seemed solid when I tapped it with my knuckles. I pried at the framing here and there. It was nailed in place, strong and tight wherever I looked, until I came to the lowest corner. The wood there was blackened and eaten away, the last inch of framework missing altogether. Another piece came loose at a tug, as though nothing gripped the

nails. The mushroom smell wafted over me with such a rich-
ness that I guessed the rot went on and on behind the panel,
maybe fully through the hull.

I didn't wait to prod any farther. The bearded man was
hidden now, but I didn't fear him. I wrapped my shirt around
the chains and crawled between the benches and out through
the door, into a deeper darkness. I kept moving, calling in a
whisper for Midgely.

Scuffling sounds made me pause, until I realized that I
was hearing rats on the deck below. I started forward again,
then wondered what had put the rats on the move.

"Midgely?" I whispered.

There was a different sound then, a small scrape and a
clink of metal. And the boy who answered wasn't Midgely.

"Nosey," he said, very softly. "Nosey, where are you?"

I went forward more quickly. When I came to a ladder, I
was no longer sure if I wanted to go down or up. But it
seemed easier to go down, and I let the chains dangle from
my feet. They settled on each rung in turn, easing their
weight for a moment, then falling away with a jerk on my
ankles.

I was nearly at the bottom when a voice said, "Don't
move."

And a hand reached out and grabbed my ankle.

fourteen
THE FARM BOY BUCKLES UNDER

The fright that I got nearly brought a scream from my lips. My hands flew from the ladder, and I barely caught it again as I went toppling backward. I clutched the rung with all my strength, but it seemed my heart had plummeted to the floor.

When I lifted my foot, someone pulled it down.

"Tom! It's me. It's Midgely." He held my chains so they could make no sound, and he told me, "Stay still!"

The nobs were above us. I heard them scuttling across the deck with that jingle of irons and the soft padding of bare feet. I heard their whispers and pressed myself against the ladder. The nobs came closer, nearly right to the hatch. Weedle called out, soft and clear, "Nosey. No-o-sey!"

They stopped right above me. The darkness was so complete that I couldn't see Midge, and I supposed they couldn't see me. But I felt the ladder tremble, as though someone was starting down. Then I heard the nobs moving, and I waited a long while before dropping down to Midgely's side.

I expected to find him lying battered and bleeding, but he was fine. He was even a little annoyed. "I've been waiting forever," he said. "Where did you go?"

"I'm not sure," I told him.

We huddled where we were, and even slept for a while on the hard deck below the ladder. Midgely, knowing the patterns of the ship, got us safely in our hammocks before the guards came below to start our day. We were marched to the deck and down again, and I thought that breakfast would follow. But we went in a different direction, toward the front of the ship, straight to the home of my bearded man.

It was the chapel. There sat my benches in their perfect rows. There, high above me, stood the silent figure. His feet crossed, his arms spread, he was carved out of wood—a crucified Jesus. As I looked at his downturned face, a small flame kindled in my heart. I felt that he would protect me, that I *would* escape from the hulk. Even that I had to.

I maneuvered to the proper bench, Midgely at my side. As we sat, the chaplain entered through a narrow door beside the altar. In a white surplice he climbed to his pulpit, opened a black Bible, and read the psalm that began "The Lord is my shepherd." The hundreds of boys sat in silence, none of them listening, all looking up at the sunlight that glistened in the barred hatch where I'd seen the sickle moon. I leaned against the wall, exploring with my foot the bit of framing near the floor. I could see the heads of the nails I'd loosened.

The chaplain closed his Bible with a thump. "Come, ye children, I will teach you the fear of the Lord," he said, raising his hands. "On your feet now. Catechisms, boys."

We stood as one and followed him through the wretched catechisms. Many a bum-brush I'd gotten in school learning those endless things, but I knew them by heart. The chaplain asked the first question, and we bleated out the answer like a herd of talking sheep. He asked the second, and the third, staring down from his pulpit to see who was talking and who was silent. In that way of all boys, most only mumbled bits of nonsense to add their voices to a babble.

I looked at the panels of wainscotting, wondering how to remove them. I wished for tools I could never have, so lost in my thoughts that I didn't hear the chaplain conclude his service. Suddenly the boys were standing, and he was staring down, pointing right at me. "That boy," he said. "*That* boy will stay behind."

When the room was empty he came down from the altar. His face was long, his forehead high, framed in white hair and white bushes of whiskers. All he needed was a red dot on the tip of his nose to be an old Silly Billy from a London fair. It wouldn't have surprised me to hear him burst out in one of those clown's little songs: "Eh, higgety, eh ho!"

But when he smiled, the image of a clown deserted me. He seemed only kindly, a small man with big wrinkles and sad eyes. "You know your catechisms well," he said. "Where did you learn them, son?"

"In church, Father," I said. "In school."

"Indeed?" His eyes brightened. They were pale and squinted, as though he needed spectacles but refused to wear them. "I meet few boys who've had schooling. Tell me; what led you astray?"

I didn't hesitate. "Mr. Goodfellow."

"Ah," said he. "Did you rob him? Did you beat him?"

"No, sir. It's what he did to *me.*"

"Now, now. The first step to salvation is confession, my

107

boy." His fingers raked through his whiskers. "Would it help you to come here in the evenings?"

"Oh, yes, sir." I could hardly believe my luck.

"I have a small library. You can read, can't you?"

I nodded. "Yes, Father."

"Splendid. I will hope you use it often." He stood up and called for a guard to take me to breakfast. "The boys are set in wicked ways, and I feel sometimes that my work is wasted here," he told me. "But you give me hope. I'd like to help you on your way."

"I believe you will, sir." I smiled back at him, but felt rather rotten inside.

When I arrived at the breakfast table the boys were on their feet for the blessing. With one look at Oten Acres, I knew who the nobs had been after in the night. His hands trembled as they held his bowl. His face was puffed and bruised, one eye blackened, lips split open. And more than that, he was broken through and through. Without a word of complaint he passed up a share of his food, then lowered his head as though he might never lift it again.

Midgely whispered at me. "He's a meek now, ain't he, Tom? He'll inherit the earth, sure as spit."

I gave up my own share as easily as Oten had done, and Weedle gloated in his power, his eyes shining. Now and then they fixed on me, and I shuddered to think what he might be planning. But I ate all that was left of my food. If Midgely expected some, he neither asked nor complained. I spooned up the slop without looking.

"Smasher," said Weedle.

I nearly answered to the name before I realized that was what he wanted. In his stupid cunning he'd hoped to trap me, to prove a truth that didn't exist.

"You're him, ain't you?" he said.

I pretended not to know that he was even talking to me.

"I'll give you what you gave me, and more," he said. "Cut my face? I'll cut your ears off, nosey. I'll slice your lips away, you'll see."

He put fear in my heart; there was no denying it. And the fear made me desperate to be gone from the ship. So it was Weedle's own fault, in a way, that I stole a needle from the workroom table. I thought it would help me dig through rotted wood, but I didn't think whose it was. I tucked it into my rope belt as I rose for our noontime meal, and learned what I'd done as soon as we sat for the afternoon.

Oten Acres picked up his needle; Midgely picked up his. Carrots and the others started sewing again, and only Weedle was left empty-handed. He sorted through his piles of cloth—lazily at first, and then frantically. He hurled the pieces aside. "Who's got my needle?" he said. "Who nicked it?"

No one even looked at him.

"Bumpkin!"

"No," said Oten, in a pathetic tone that I would hardly have known was his. "It weren't me, Weedle, I swear it."

"Give me yours," said Weedle. "Carrots, hurry. Take it from him."

It was too late for that. A guard came running, and the fuss that was made over a missing needle would have shocked me just days before. Weedle was caned on the back, then marked for punishment in the morning. "Someone's going to pay for this," he said. "Someone's going to wish he wasn't never born."

His needle stayed in my belt until the evening, when I went to chapel with the noseys, a lot of pale and scared-looking boys. Every table in the ship, I realized, must have had a Weedle to keep the weaker boys downtrodden. They were half starved and scurvy-ridden, coughing with the fever, all as thin as death. They fell aside like so many sticks as I pushed my way to the rotted wood. I brought out the needle when the chaplain made us kneel to prayers. I poked it into the rotted wood, half its length in an instant. With a bit of effort I pushed it nearly to its eye.

Chanting my prayers with the others, I worked the needle in and out in the same spot. Then I bent forward, as though in great reverence, and with my cheek nearly on the deck I looked for a gleam of light in the hole I'd made. I was sure the hull was no thicker than the length of my needle.

I left it there when prayers ended, its whole length buried in the wood. Only the tip was showing, a bump of brown metal nearly impossible to see. *"All but invisible,"* I remembered Midgely saying, and surprised myself with my fondness for him. But as I was leaving the room, the chaplain stopped me. To my relief, he wanted only to thank me. "It's not often that a boy shows interest in prayer," he said. "You must have a probing mind." I almost felt sorry for the old codger.

Midgely was waiting when I went into the ward. Weedle was there too, in his usual place with his usual group, and every one of them watched me pass with the noseys. I looked at them once, and then away, going straight to Midgely's side. He was studying the pictures of his South Sea islands, so deeply immersed in the etching that he started when I touched his shoulder. Then he smiled and asked me to sit beside him.

"I decided it don't matter," he said.

"What do you mean?" I asked.

"If you want to go to chapel with the noseys. It ain't no odds to me." He shrugged, then held the book toward me. "Read to me, Tom?" he said.

In the crowd of boys we made our own small space. I had no worries with the guards around, and sat shoulder to shoulder with Midge, the book balanced on our knees. I found a passage about a ship and its sailors, and Midge closed his eyes to listen. To me it was jibberish. "We dropped the best bower and veered off on a cable and a half," I read. "Struck yards and topmasts. Rove out cable for the cooper."

"Ooh," said Midge, with a shiver that shook the pages. "It musht have been a shtormy night."

"It doesn't say that," I said. "You're not listening."

"You're not *hearing*," he said, and explained it all. I didn't know that bowers were anchors, that a cable was both a rope and a distance. I didn't know that yards were the sticks that held the sails, or that sections of masts could be lowered and raised. But Midge made me see. He turned the dull words into pictures of excitement, with sailors bustling about like so many bees.

"How do you know all that?" I asked.

"From the dockyard," he said. "Every night the sailors came to see me mam. She loved to have the sailors come and visit. They took turns going into the bedroom to talk to her, Tom. So I sat in the parlor with the ones what waited, and I listened to their stories. Ooh, what stories they told."

It was the time in the evening when the guards let us talk. But we did it in whispers, our heads close together.

"Where was your father?" I asked.

"Oh, he was long gone," said Midge. "But he was a captain, I think. I remember he had a sword."

"So did mine," I said. "My father's a captain, too."

"Go on!" he said. "You're just saying it 'cause I said it first."

"No, it's true," I said. "But the navy has no place for him now. He hasn't had a ship in years, and—"

"Tin? You don't mean *Redman* Tin?" said Midge. "Not Redman Tin what had the *Starling*?"

It was my father's name, but the rest was a mystery. "Was the starling a bird or a ship?" I asked.

"Wal-ker!" he said, just like old Worms. "She was only a sloop. Only ten guns. And Redman Tin weren't really a captain; he was a commander. But when Nelson seen what your dad could do with them ten guns, he called that sloop his darling. And listen, Tom, he was here." Midge tapped the wooden deck. "Your dad was on this ship."

"No! He was never on a *hulk,*" I said.

"Oh, Tom!" he cried with a laugh. "The *Lachesis* weren't always a hulk. She was at the Glorious First of June, Tom. Your father was a young midshipman on her, and she chased the French right back to Brest. He was a hero in the wars, Tom. All the sailors, they still remember Redman Tin."

I knew little of my father's years at sea. After Kitty's death, my mother had hushed him quickly whenever he had begun to talk of it. *"Look where the sea brought you,"* she'd say. *"To rack and ruin. Don't turn the boy's head."* After a while, he never talked of it at all. And my friends never thought of wars that had been fought long ago.

"Your dad knew Collingwood," said Midge. "He might have met Nelson." Then he stared at me from the corner of his eye. "Why, he might have come and talked to me mam."

When the guards locked us down we cleared out on our own, away from the seething Weedle. I didn't want to go to the chapel that night, afraid that his nobs would follow me, or find me there. Instead, I followed Midgely through the ship to a place that he wanted to show me. It was dark and cramped, with the ceiling very low. In the wars, said Midge, this was where the midshipmen had lived among their sea chests, where they'd slept and dined and studied.

We settled in the darkest corner, and heard the nobs go roaming. Huddled on the bare floor, Midge and I slept the night through, on the same ship where my father had slept thirty-four years before.

fifteen

MIDGELY HAS HIS DOUBTS

Weedle's punishment was swift and terrible. I watched him being led from the workroom in the morning, and not ten minutes later I heard him cry out in pain. Twelve times came the whistle and crack of a whip, and then that sound like a frightened dog. I winced at every one.

So did Midgely, at my side. His hands twitched; his needle leapt in the cloth. "The cat," he whispered. "He's getting the *cat.*"

The cat-o'-nine-tails; even I knew of that. It must have torn the flesh from Weedle's back, but he was brought straight to the table within the hour, and put to work again. He sat then, and for the days to follow, in an awkward fashion, so that his back never touched a chair. The look in his eyes was of savage hatred, and they bore on me more than any other.

It occurred to me that I was more than a match for him

then. He was so weakened, and in such pain, that I might have thrashed him if I'd dared to try. But it wasn't in me to fight with anyone. I'd been raised to be a gentleman, with a horror for fisticuffs.

At least I was free from Weedle. He sweated and groaned through the day, then took to his hammock as though he would never leave it. As Carrots and the other nobs huddled round him like wet nurses, I led Midgely to the chapel. I took my spoon and bowl, and made Midge take his, and we crouched by the rotted wood, below the crucified Jesus.

Midgely wasn't happy to be there. "Do you think it's right, digging in a chapel?" he said. "It ain't like burning a Bible, is it?"

"Not for me," I said. "I shouldn't be on the ship anyway, Midge. I'm innocent."

"Yes, me too," he said, with a sudden cheerfulness. "Or I'm halfway innocent. Where's the harm in buffing dogs?"

"What's buffing dogs?" I asked.

"Only a dodge, Tom," he said. "You sell their skins, you see. You stick a wire in them. Here." He jabbed his finger at my chest. "It goes right to their heart and does them in as gentle as you please. They lick your hand when you do it, Tom. Like they're thanking you. They lie there and lick your hand, then off to sleep they go. And you know, Tom, they're lucky, I think. No more begging, no more beatings. Sometimes I wish someone had buffed me three years ago."

"Is that how long you've been here?" I asked.

"Three years at Christmas."

I didn't want to think about any of that, not the poor dogs licking his hand as they died, nor Midgely wasting his life in a hulk. I patted his hand, and turned away. "Look," I said, showing him the nails I had loosened, the rot at the foot of the panel. He had to peer and squint in the darkness, but his eyes widened when I pulled the needle from its hiding place. "Oh, Tom. You'll catch it now," he said. "If Weedle sees that, you're a goner."

"I'll be a goner long before then," I said dryly. "I'll be gone from here in just a few days."

We took off the framing, pulling each piece—nails and all—from the oak. We pried the panel away and set it aside, baring the rot underneath. Midgely whistled softly. "The poor old ship," he said. "She don't deserve to rot like this."

The planks were soft and mushy, with that warm smell of mushrooms and earth like a wonderful perfume. Using our spoons, we dug the wood away, scraping a hole as wide as my shoulders. We piled the pieces in our bowls, but soon overfilled them. The wood was so soft that it fell away in chunks.

"How thick are these planks?" I asked.

"Tom, they ain't *planks,*" said Midge. "It's called the quickwork, and it's—"

"I don't care what it's *called,*" I said. "How thick is it, Midge?"

"Three or four inches," said he. "But, Tom—"

"Shut up and dig," I told him.

Poor Midge. He fell silent then, and sulked until dawn. Even without his help I was more than pleased with my progress that night. When we fitted the panel in place and tapped the framing on top, we hid a hole that went a third of the way through the planks. We gathered the scraps—a great pile of black shreds—and dumped them out through a grating. But in the daylight, at morning chapel, I was shocked at the sight of scores of black flakes scattered across the wood like so many dead flies. I scraped them into a pile with my feet, then pushed them close against the wall.

The chaplain never noticed. Again he unwittingly helped me along when I asked if I might clean the chapel instead of scrubbing floors. He was delighted, but not so much as I. There, under his very nose, I swept away all signs of my work.

The very next night we broke through the planks. I could scarcely believe it happened so quickly, but I pried with my spoon, and out came a piece of wood the size of a small book. Its sides were as jagged as all the others, but its back was flat and smooth—the outside of the plank.

"Midge!" I cried. "Look, Midge, we've done it!"

I thrust my hand into the hole, but my fingers only jammed against more wood. "What's wrong?" I said. "Is there another ship tied up to this one?"

Midge laughed. "That's the frames back there," he said. "This is just the quickwork, Tom; I told you that. There's still the frames and planks to go."

It was a great disappointment. I'd thought I'd be off the ship that night or the next, but it seemed I had only begun. "How thick is the hull?" I asked. "The whole thing, I mean?"

"Only thick enough to stop a cannonball," said Midge.

"And how thick's *that*?" I snapped. "From inside to out, how thick is it, Midge?"

In the darkness he held his hands apart. He moved them back and forth to measure the distance, and I groaned when he stopped. Maybe ten inches; maybe a foot. And the wood in the frames seemed hard as stone. "It's as thick as your head," I told him.

"Don't say that, Tom." He bit his lip, then started sobbing. "I think Weedle'sh maybe right. What he saysh might be true. You really are the Shmasher."

"Oh, Midge," I said. "I'm sorry." But I had no patience for him. I went to work with my needle, poking at the frames of the ship. It scratched the wood, but nothing more. I saw that I would sooner bend the needle than split the timbers, and, disheartened, I threw it down. It *plink*ed against the deck, then *plink*ed again more faintly in the distance. In the darkness of the huge chapel it might as well have landed in a haystack.

Midge hurried to fetch it, but I'd lost hope. I sat there like an old hermit in front of his cave, my arms around my knees, the heavy irons piled between my feet. I couldn't dig through a ship with a needle and spoon; I'd been stupid to try at all.

"Found it," cried Midge, in a whisper. He came scuttling back. "Here's your needle, Tom."

"It's no good," I said. "I need something bigger, something . . ."

I looked up, toward the hatch, toward the wooden man below it. His face was barely touched by starlight, his eyes like black holes. I couldn't see his feet or his hands.

I got up and shuffled toward the altar. Midge, still holding the needle out to me, said, "Tom? What are you doing?"

Up the stairs I went, in a rumble of scraping irons. Even at the top I couldn't reach the bearded man, and had to climb higher, on spindles and knobs of wood, nearly right to the hatch, where the stars shone pale and yellow.

"Tom?" said Midge. "Have you gone off your nut?"

I balanced on a narrow ledge and, reaching up, grasped the feet of the crucified Jesus. With my face pressed against the wall, I couldn't look up. My knees trembled at the effort of standing there, stretching full length as I was, to touch the wooden toes and then the wooden ankles. The spike that went through them was metal.

Midgely drew a breath when he realized what I was doing. I heard it clearly, his gasp from far below. "Oh, Tom," he said. "No. You can't do that."

The spike was fitted snugly in a hole. I thought for a moment that it wouldn't come loose, but it did. I drew it out inch by inch, then nearly dropped it when it came suddenly free. Heavy and thick, it was fully eight inches long.

It was harder to go down than up. With the spike tucked into my belt, I had to feel for every handhold, every place to set my feet. I was nearly out of breath when I reached the floor, but still went straight to work. Where before I had taken out only slivers and flakes of wood, I now tore away finger-sized chunks. Still, I could see that the job would take many more nights than I'd hoped.

But as the days went by, and Weedle grew stronger, I became more desperate. Midgely was loathe to use the spike, or even to touch it at first. I pleaded and bargained, yet it did no good.

"Why should I help you, Tom?" he asked one night, looking pathetically sad. "I don't want you to go. Why should I help you get away?"

"Because I'll take you," I said.

"Honest?"

"Of course. I always meant to take you with me." It was a lie, but he believed it. He asked where we would go and what we would do. "Well, what would you like?" I said.

He thought for a moment, biting his lip. "To go to Ireland," he told me. "It would be dead easy, Tom. We could walk to Bristol, then steal a boat and cross the sea to Ireland. We'd be safe there forever."

"Then that's what we'll do," I said. Another lie. Crossing the sea in a stolen boat was the last thing I would do. In truth, I would leave Midge on the marshes as soon as we escaped. I would leave him sleeping in the rushes like the baby Moses in his Bible book. But of course I didn't tell him that, and he didn't suspect it.

Our work went on with a pleasing speed. There were times when I saw Midge chipping away in the darkness and thought of my sister, Kitty, who had been about the same size when she died. In those moments I imagined I might take him along. But I soon thought better of it. He was too young and too small; he would only slow me down. Yet I imagined the disappointment he would feel when I left him. I nearly felt it myself. I pitied him then, and that annoyed me greatly.

I made it up to him as best as I could. Hours and hours we spent studying his book of the South Seas. I felt as though I'd joined a ship that went sailing through the pages, from island to island. Groups of black natives came paddling out in great canoes to welcome us with baskets full of fruit. Like Midge, I found myself slipping into the pictures, into the story. I saw that he had found his own way of escaping from the wretched *Lachesis*. He had no need to tunnel from the hulk; he was already outside it, more free—in a fashion—than I could ever hope to be. The idea made me envious at first, and then frightened. Could a person lose his mind in imaginary islands?

The feeling came so strongly one night that I suddenly closed the book. It was like closing a window on a different world, and all there was to see again was the ship and the pitiful boys. Midgely tried to pry it open again. "Don't stop," he said.

"I don't want to read anymore," I told him.

"Then we can look at the pictures," he said.

"No." I kept it shut. "When you go outside, up on deck, what do you see, Midge?"

He frowned. "What do you *think* I see?"

"Palm trees," I said. "I think you see jungles and sandy beaches."

"Not likely!" He laughed. "I see a ship, Tom. But not an old hulk. I see a ship of the line like she used to be. Them shacks is gone, and all her sails is set, and I'm a sailor working the ship." He gazed up at me, and in the depth of his feelings his words became more slurred. "Oh, Tom, I don't care if we ever get out. I want to be transhported. I want it sho badly. Every day, more than anything, that'sh what I want."

"To be *transported*?"

"Yes. To get beyond the sheash." He nuzzled even closer. "I can't hardly wait for that."

"But the ship's half rotten," I said. "And the masts are cut off."

He frowned, then laughed again. "Oh, we won't go in *this*," he said. "They'll put us on a proper ship. And now's the time, when it's summer in the south. We have to round the Cape of Good Hope in the summer."

The Cape of Good Hope! It was the one place my father had been allowed to talk about. The weather was so wretched, the place so terrible, that my mother had delighted in its horrors. "Tell the boy about the Cape," she'd say. "Tell him about the storms. Tell him about the ghost ship." My father had seen it there, the *Flying Dutchman,* tearing along with its sails in rags, its crew all skeletons and corpses.

"The Cape of Storms, they call it," said Midgely. "Look here; I'll show you."

He pulled at the book, and I gave it up. He opened it almost at the very page he wanted, a picture of monstrous waves, with the only land a mere scratch in the distance. Across the picture ran a ship, a great ship with sails as small as handkerchiefs. Nearly all the deck was underwater, and the sailor who was steering was lashed to the wooden wheel. The ship lay nearly on its side, and the next wave rolling toward it—breaking at the top into foam and spray—was taller than the masts. Below the picture, the writing said "Summer off the Cape."

I was doomed. If Regent's Pond on a sunny day could set my knees shaking, what would the ocean do? I had to get off the ship. I had to go soon.

Sixteen
A VERY NASTY SCHEME

Oten Acres was dying. He wasn't the only one; all around that miserable ship the weaker boys were fading away. Two mornings in a row, there was another who never got out of his hammock. The guards came and bundled them in the canvas, then carried them up to the sunshine.

But Oten didn't have the fever like them. He didn't have scurvy or wasting disease, yet he was surely dying. I knew it at breakfast one day, when I saw how he stared at the grating. My mother had worn just the same look when she'd sat for endless hours gazing at the little altar she'd made for Kitty. It was as though, inside, he was already dead.

It was several days after his beating. The bruises on his face were still bright and lurid. Blood had dried round his mouth in brown cakes, in his hair like rusted cables, but he hadn't bothered to wash it away. He sat absolutely still, huge and hunched, gazing toward that grid of bars.

He didn't eat his food anymore. Every boy at every meal eyed it with lip-licking greed, and even I fancied a share. I, who owned riches beyond belief, wanted nothing more than a bite of Oten's moldy bread. As soon as we rose from the benches, it seemed a flock of seagulls descended on the table. The farm boy's food disappeared in a tangle of reaching hands, and was torn apart in the struggle.

We put away the tables and benches. I started toward the chapel, but stopped when I saw Oten rubbing his scrubbing brush in circles, still staring at the window.

"Ain't nothing you can do for him," said Midgely, coming to my side. "Those boys from the country never last long. They die like the grass." He nodded. "Like grass without sun."

It didn't sound like Midgely to phrase it that way. I imagined he was parroting what someone else had told him—maybe the kindly old chaplain. But he was certainly brokenhearted. "They do, Tom," he said. "They don't even *try* to hang on. And it don't help to worry about them."

I *wasn't* worried, though it shamed me to admit it. My only worry was Weedle, who was getting strong very quickly now. He knew that every night I left my hammock, so how long could it be before he learned where I went?

It nearly happened that very night, as Midge and I were digging. We were halfway through the frames by then, and Midge was picking at the wood in his fussy way when he suddenly turned toward me. "Tom?" he said. "When we get out, what will we do?"

"I've been thinking of that," I told him. "They'll bring soldiers, I think."

He nodded. "And dogs. We'll have to look sharp to keep ahead of them."

"Well, that's where you're wrong," I said. "We'll keep *behind* them, Midge." I pried at a sliver he'd loosened. "We'll bury ourselves in the mud, so close to the ship that they won't even look where we are. Then, when they're searching for us miles away, we'll slip off toward London."

Midgely whistled. "That's a wicked plan, Tom."

But you won't be going, I thought. Poor Midge.

"That's a plan and a half," he said. "But, Tom? What will we do when we get out of the ship and fall in the water?"

I stopped working. I hadn't even thought of the river beyond the planks. In all my imaginings I had gone straight from the ship to the marsh, never thinking of water between them.

"Is the river deep?" I asked.

"Hookey Walker! The ship's floating, ain't she?"

It would be fathoms deep. I would drop like an anchor through the cold water, past the weeds and the fishes. My irons would raise puffs of mud as they were buried in the bottom, and there I would stay forever.

"I was thinking," said Midge. "We'll have to go on the springs, Tom. She'll set her garboards down then."

I hated sailor talk. "Say what you mean," I snapped. "What are garboards? What are springs?"

"The garboards are the bottom planks," he said patiently. "Springs are the big tides that come after the full moon, and in December they're biggest of all. She'll settle right into the mud then. Why, we could nearly walk to shore."

"Underwater?"

"I can hold my breath forever. Look, Tom." He suddenly filled his lungs in one gasp, then sat there with his eyes closed, his cheeks puffed out.

I ignored him. All my life I had had nightmares of falling in water. Countless times I had woken kicking from those dreams, breathless and choked, so drenched in sweat that I might indeed have been underwater. I couldn't even imagine dropping into the dark river, or crawling across its bottom, through the mud and weeds, past the crabs and the worms and whatever else there might be. The moment the water closed over my head, my mind would unhinge like my mother's. But I had to try; I had to get off the ship. If I wasn't killed by Weedle I would wither away like Oten Acres, and either way I would be carried from the ship in a brown bundle.

I looked up at the hatch. The moon was a white sickle, half hidden by clouds. I didn't know if it was waxing or waning, or how many nights would pass before it came full, but the springs were surely coming.

"Midge, I have to get my irons taken off," I said.

He let out his breath with a startling *puff!* His face was red. "See that, Tom?" he said proudly.

I didn't care how long he could hold his breath. "Tell me how to get my irons off," I said.

"You can't," said he.

"But the Overseer told me . . ."

Midge laughed. "He told *me* that, too. He tells everyone that. He only wants you to be a meek, is all."

"What about the list?" I said. "The liberty list."

"It might be true," said Midge with a shrug. "But I never seen it happen. When the ship gets crowded they pack boys off, that's all I know. I seen whole bunches go, but not me. If you ain't thirteen, or wicked as the devil, they don't care how long you stay."

"I'm older than that," I said.

"Lucky you." He sounded jealous. "They might transport you any day."

I didn't want that. With nearly four hundred boys on the ship, how much more crowded could it be?

The moon went gliding by and the clouds filled in, and the chapel grew blacker than ever. We worked by feel alone, chipping away at the massive frames. For another hour we labored together; then I slept while Midge carried on. "We've no time to waste. You'll have to keep at it," I told him. But when I woke hours later, he had taken out no more wood than could fill a thimble.

"It was the nobs," he said. "Them and Weedle, they came looking for us."

"I don't believe you," I said. "Weedle isn't strong enough yet."

"Might have fooled me," said Midge. "I know what you think, Tom. That I'm a lazy twiddlepoop, but I'm not."

"Well, you're not any *help,*" I told him. "I'd do better by myself."

"You think so, Tom?"

"Yes," I said.

Without another word he picked up his irons and shuffled away, around the benches and out the door. I thought he would be back in a moment, shamed into working harder than ever. I took up the spike, drove it at the frames, and with a crack and a groan, a splinter came out. It was smaller than my thumb, but more than Midge had managed in all the time I'd slept. I pushed and pried with the spike, hammered and pulled, until I had to stop from sheer exhaustion. Then, panting heavily, I felt a deep despair. The hulk had already taken its toll on my strength.

I looked up, trying to pick out the shape of the wooden Jesus, to find again the hope he'd given me. But he was so hidden by darkness that he might not have been there at all.

"Oh, please," I whispered. "Please help me." I cried out to that wooden figure, begging for another chance to see my father, to hold my mother, to claim my lost riches.

As I talked he appeared. It may have been the light from the stars, in a sudden parting of the clouds. But he seemed to step out from the darkness. Bearded and sad, he emerged from the shadows, and perhaps for a minute he stood there still and quiet before he slipped away again.

I went back to my work. I pulled away chunks of wood, and suddenly that wonderful smell came wafting from the hole. Just beyond where I'd stopped, the frames were mushy and rotten. With my hands I tore them apart.

Then I heard the footsteps. They came steadily along the deck, heavy steps that marched with a rhythm. It wasn't Midgely, and it couldn't be Weedle. It was someone with boots, coming with a purpose, as though sent to help. I left the panel open, my poor tools strewn around, and moved out through the chapel door. The long deck looked empty, but I heard the footsteps marching, and then the warble of a whistled tune—"Adeste Fideles," that lovely hymn.

There was a flare of light, a swoop of shadows. Thirty paces away, the ladder that led up to the workrooms glowed in a yellow fire. I might not have been surprised to see the spirit of my father come down in that light. But it was only a guard who appeared, a lantern in one hand, a sturdy cane in the other.

The light seemed to spread up the deck. It flashed into hidden spaces, onto the shapes of boys crouched by the timbers.

"Who's there?" cried the guard. He raised his lantern.

The boys leapt up. They rushed the guard from either side. His whistling stopped, and the lantern shattered on the deck, its light instantly extinguished to all but a smoldering wick. Then locks rattled, and deep voices called down from the decks above. I heard Weedle shout, "Clear off!" The boys scattered, and the guard went running.

I watched them go, then hurried to the place where the guard had fallen. I gathered bits of the broken glass, then found his cane—or half of it—lying at the foot of the ladder.

Hatches had opened, and cold air swirled through the ship. With pounding steps and booming voices, other guards were coming. But the first to reach me was Midge, hobbling from the darkness with his chains in his hands. "Tom!" he cried. "What are you doing?"

"Look for the cane," I said. I had a plan, but no time to tell him what it was.

seventeen
OTEN SMELLS THE FIELDS

We found the rest of the cane against the wall. We threw the two halves and some pieces of glass into the hole and replaced the panel. As the guards came pounding down the ladders, we put the framing in place. The lights from their lanterns were flashing through the ship when we fled from the chapel.

Midgely was faster than I. His irons rattling, he ran ahead while I struggled with mine. I tripped and rose again, then tumbled down a ladder. A guard came right behind, and I reached my hammock only just in time. I settled into it as the space filled with light and guards.

I turned toward Midge, eager to see if he was safely there. I reached across and shook the ropes that held his hammock. "Midge?" I whispered.

A face rose from the canvas. But it wasn't Midgely's. I looked straight into Weedle's dark eyes.

"I know where you go," he said. "Don't think you're safe hiding in a chapel. I got a score to settle, I do. And it don't bother me where it's done."

With that he turned away. His irons clinked as he rolled over in the hammock. I lay still, staring at the ceiling, thankful for the guards. They stayed with us till daylight, tramping up and down as a storm began to rise. It came in a whistle of wind, a shiver in the hull. The hammocks swayed in that long sort of ripple that had sickened me before. And hour by hour the storm grew worse.

I didn't see Midge until morning chapel. He slipped into the bench at my side, looking worried and worn. In a whisper, as the benches filled, he said that Weedle had taken his hammock before he could get there. "He knows everything, Tom," he said. "But, Tom, I didn't tell him."

"I know that," I said. "He's going to come after me, Midge."

In the roof of the chapel, above the crucified figure, the rain tapped on the hatch like hundreds of tiny hammers. The chaplain had to raise his voice above the sound of the wind in the rigging. I could hear waves drumming on the hull.

By the hour it worsened. The ship groaned; it creaked. The rain fell so heavily that there might have been herds of hoofed animals trampling the deck above the workroom. Our reels of thread rolled back and forth, the lamps swung wildly, and I felt even sicker than I had on my first day. As we marched to our noontime meal I staggered like a drunken sot. And in my weakness, Weedle must have seen his chance.

At the mouth of the hatch, he came at me. With a cry and a leap he was there. Suddenly I was falling to the deck and he was on top of me, his fist in my hair. From his clothing he pulled a piece of glass that was long and thin like a dagger's blade. He raised it up and drove it down toward my throat.

I wasn't strong enough to throw him off me. I wriggled sideways and jerked my neck, and Weedle missed by less than an inch. The glass dug into the deck. I heard its tip crunch and crackle, a little grunt from Weedle as his hand slipped along its edge. When he held it up again there was blood dripping from his palm, streaming down the glass. His scar twisted across his face. "Cut me?" he said. "I'll cut your throat." And again he stabbed that thing toward me.

I moved the other way; I turned my head. With a fizz of a sound, the glass sizzled through my hair. It broke against the deck and went skittering in little pieces across the wood. I felt Weedle's breath as he snarled and swore. At last the guards hauled him off, and down to the black hole went Weedle. There was no question how he had found that piece of glass. It could only have come from the guard's broken lantern. Straight to the hole he was taken.

I shouted after him, the worst thing I could think of just then. "You snow smugger!" I cried, and poor Midge turned as white as a pile of salt.

"Oh, no, Tom," he said. "You shouldn't have said that. He'll know I told you."

"It doesn't matter anymore," I said. "He's finished."

"You don't know him, Tom. You don't know him at all."

Well, I thought I did, and I felt free just then. But still I couldn't eat my supper, not with the ship all ashiver in waves that boomed at the hull. Spray from the river flew in through the grates, and the wind was an endless screech. I sat feeling dry as dust in my innards, but with sweat pouring on my skin. The low ceiling pressed toward me.

Midgely said, "Think of Nelson, Tom. He was seasick all the time."

"Anchored in a river?" I asked.

He almost giggled. "Maybe not *all* the time."

Toward the end of the day, in our last hour of sewing, there was a sort of thump, then a rattle in the timbers. Midgely looked up. "Feel that, Tom?" he said. "She touched."

My mouth was too dry to speak.

"The wind's driving her toward the bank," whispered Midge. "If it's like this in the springs, she'll nearly be ashore."

"How long?" I asked.

"Maybe a week," said Midge. "Not more than ten days."

"And how long will Weedle be in the hole?"

He shrugged. "No one's never been there more than a week."

Our time was short. But that night I couldn't possibly shift myself from my hammock. I held on as it swayed back and forth, nearly wishing for death to find me. Nothing could be worse than the seasickness. "Is there no way to stop this?" I asked.

"Nelson said you should sit under a tree," said Midge. He laughed at the cleverness of his stupid hero. "It goes away, Tom. You just have to wait."

It was the storm that went away. It passed with the dawn, and left the seagulls whirling in great squawking pinwheels of white. The wind fell away. The waves settled down, and my stomach settled with them, and that night we set to work with a will.

As Midge tunneled in the chapel, I took the guard's broken cane and carefully split each piece down the middle. I scraped them hollow with a shard of his lantern glass, then rejoined the halves. I bound them round and round with strands from my rope belt. I sealed them with tar that I scraped from the hull. When I put one end in my mouth and raised the other, Midgely grinned to see what I'd made. "We can breathe through those," he said. "Oooh, that's lummy, Tom."

The days passed quickly. Storm followed storm, but each one sickened me a little less. My mind wandered easily from the workroom as I imagined myself back in London, finding my father and setting him free, unearthing my diamond and spending its riches. I regretted more than ever that Midge would be left behind, and I was pleased that he never guessed it.

We still took out his books and traveled to his islands. All around us, boys played their games of pitch-button and French and English—that battle fought on pickaback—as we met the black-skinned natives in their villages of huts. The ship was a better place without Walter Weedle.

We sometimes heard him at night. The black hole was below us, and not far away, and we heard him at first shouting and cursing and hammering at the wood. As the days went by he began to wail, then howl like a hound. Sometimes, in the quiet of the night's middle passage, as the ship slept and I worked, I heard his voice shouting my name from the depths of his hole. "I know where you are! I'll kill you, Tom Tin."

There were boys who delighted in Weedle's being gone. Even some of his little gang seemed pleased, for they had no one to rob them of their meals. But much to my surprise, Oten Acres found no relief. The big farm boy kept wilting, shriveling, until he could barely turn himself from his hammock. He never ate, and I didn't believe he ever slept. If someone addressed him, he didn't answer. He stared into nothing with eyes so vacant that I sometimes doubted he even knew where he was. I saw him one morning wandering on the deck, his irons dragging as he plodded in the line. He was so hunched, so bent and broken, that the rain fell on his back, barely wetting his shoulders. It was as though he had resigned himself to death, and was only waiting for it to come.

It was Weedle's fourth night in the hole when we reached the planks behind the frames. It was the night the moon came full, though clouds kept it hidden. The wind was high, the river wild, and we could hear Weedle howling below us. I felt the hulk swing toward the marshes. With a shudder and a bang, it settled heavily into the mud, then leaned slowly on its side. At breakfast we had to hold on to our bowls to save them from sliding off the table. Everywhere we walked we seemed to go at a slant, until, halfway through the morning—and with the most unearthly groans—the ship finally picked itself up from the bottom.

It did it again the next night, when Midge and I were in the chapel. Midge said the tides must be at their lowest, and that if we didn't escape within the next two nights, it would be half a year before they were again so much in our favor.

"Then we'd better hurry," I said.

"Or maybe not," said Midge. "I was thinking, Tom. Maybe we should sit it out."

It was just like him to suggest such a thing. We were near the end of our night's work, collecting the shavings and splinters of wood. The winter nights had become so long we were doing even that in darkness.

"We have to try," I said.

"But what if we can't get out?" asked Midge. "What if we make just one little hole all the way through?"

I saw what he meant. A hole too small would be worse than none. It would be discovered, our work ruined.

"The planks are rotten," I said. The wood we had taken away was black and spongy, reeking of rot. "We must be nearly through."

"But maybe not," said Midge. "You can't tell in the dark. I wish I could see them, Tom."

"All right," I said. "I'll let you see."

I took him to clean the chapel that morning. I loosened the frames and the panel. But the old chaplain, with the worst of luck, chose that day to come back to the chapel from wherever it was he went. If he had waited another moment, he would have found us with the panel open. But he had no idea what I was doing.

He sniffed, his nose wrinkling. "It smells musty in here, Tom," he said. It was the rot he was smelling. "I wish there were a window; I wish there were an opening somewhere."

He turned away, hemming and hawing, looking all around the chapel. Tilting his head back, he looked up to the height of the altar. Then he scratched his white hair. "Tom?"

"Yes, sir?" I said.

"Do you notice something strange about our Lord?"

My heart fell. I went to his side and stared up at the wooden man.

"His ankles," said the chaplain. He was squinting like a mole, his front teeth showing. "Am I not seeing properly? Has our spike fallen out?"

"I don't think it has fallen out, Father," I said.

"Hmmm. Curious!" said he. "The shadows, perhaps."

He seemed satisfied with that, but not wholly. He bent forward and walked stooped around the room, peering under benches. I had to leave the panel as it was, very slightly ajar, until morning prayers came round, and the chapel filled with boys. The ship was resting partly on the riverbed. Its angle held the panel in place, and leaned the boys together as they sat along the benches. I was in my place, with Midge beside me and the clanking line of convicts passing, when suddenly one boy keeled over. Wan and sickly, he teetered on his heels for a moment, put his hand to his brow, and crashed to the floor. There he lay, twitching and shaking, with his eyes rolled up, his tongue a red bulge.

All the boys stood up to gawk. A pair of guards came bashing through them. And I grabbed Midgely by the shoulder.

I hauled him close and cracked the panel open. "Quick!" I said. "Take a look, but quick."

It took him only an instant. He reached inside, then fell to his place next to me, and I could tell by his face that the news wasn't good. "Tom, we're not halfway," he said. "It's another three or four nights."

I reached into the hole. The earthy smell came out, that sweetly pungent odor.

Right in front of me, Oten Acres stood up. He was round-shouldered now, and bony. He stood as all the others sat, turning around with his big, plow-hardened hands spread open. "Fields!" he said, in a terrible moan of longing. "I smell the fields."

His eyes were hollow, his cheeks sunken. He turned full around and gazed at the open panel.

"The earth," he moaned. "The fields."

I pulled Midge aside and jammed the panel shut. But I wasn't quick enough that Oten didn't see the hole behind it. He was clambering over the bench, and already three guards were pushing toward him. The little boy lay twitching on the deck, but it was Oten Acres everyone was after.

"The fields," he said again, in that haunted voice. "Let me see the fields."

The guards knocked him down. Oten put up his hands to shield himself, but the guards battered him down to his knees. We heard their grunted breaths, and Oten's cries, and the wooden Jesus stared down upon us all.

I thought the beating would be the farm boy's death. He slumped on his bench all through the service, sinking lower and lower, as though settling into his grave. But as we filed from the chapel, he came to his feet like a bull, pushing toward me. He grabbed my arm with more strength than I had ever had. "Help me, Tom," he said.

There was no pulling my arm from his grasp, no pushing him away. I couldn't even pry his fingers loose.

"I know," he said, his eyes like a madman's. "If you don't take me with you, I'll turn you in."

I had no choice. That night, for the first time, three of us went to the chapel. I was terrified that Oten would spend the time as he spent all his time, rocking and moaning until a guard came round to find us. But as soon as the panel was opened and he smelled the rot again, he went to work with such a fever that I wished I had brought him the first night.

He dug with his hands, with his fingers, clawing at the wood, then slashing at the hull with the spike. Big pieces of planks fell away. Damp and riddled with holes, they felt like the honeycombs of giant bees.

Midge had a look. "Shipworms, Tom," he said. "That's what it is." They had eaten tunnels through the planks. They'd gone back and forth through the wood, lining their holes with thin, brittle shells. "It might be like this all the way through," he said.

I was so happy that I hugged him. But he only pulled away. "Don't you see?" he said. "The worms live in the water, Tom. They swim around until they find a ship, then dig themselves into the planks."

"What does it matter where they live?" I said. "I just . . ." Then I understood. "We're digging underwater."

Midgely sighed.

"When we break through, the river will come pouring in on top of us."

"Maybe, Tom. Maybe not." He shrugged. "The ship's higher in the water now, 'cause she ain't got all her guns and spars and all. But is she high enough? I don't know."

There was no doubt that the wetness in the wood came from the river. But we wouldn't know if the surface was above us or below us until the moment we broke through the hull. And that moment, I decided, would come the very next night.

I went to breakfast feeling hopeful—perhaps more hopeful than I should have. With three of us at work, we could dig through the worm-eaten planks in an hour. If all went well, this would be my last breakfast on the ship.

The decks were at a slant, the gray burgoo at a slant in the bowls. A little rush of my old discomfort came over me, until I saw Weedle sitting at the table, just returned from the black hole. He was like his own ghost, so thin and pale he was. Yet anger oozed from his every pore, and his eyes never left me. There was only one thing that could possibly make him hate me any more than he already did. And that one thing happened right then.

eighteen
HOW MY TROUBLES DEEPEN

My back was toward the door when the guards arrived, bringing new boys. Weedle was the first to look up. Then others did, and all did. Mouths hung open, eyes stared, and I turned around in my place.

At the foot of the ladder, twisted and strange in the shadows, stood Benjamin Penny. On his awful, lopsided face was a look of fear. Then he saw me and cried one word. "Smashy!"

It was as though he led the guard to my side. Hunched and scuttling, he came like a dog on a leash to squirm up against me. His webbed fingers closed on my arm. "Smashy," he said again. "Ain't it a quiz, we fix up together?"

It was more than a *quiz*. It was a dreadful bit of luck for me. Weedle's hands were in fists, his eyes blazing hatred. "So it is you," he snarled. "You'll come a croaker now, you lying nosey, you toad."

His quiet fury stunned the boys. From Oten right around the table they sat still as wooden dolls. Midgely, on my right, seemed bewildered and betrayed. He kept looking past me at Benjamin Penny.

Penny piped up. "If I was you, Walter Weedle, I'd watch my tongue." He nudged me. "Tell him, Smashy. You'll finish what you started. Cut his mug clean in two."

Midgely tugged my arm. "Who's that?" he whispered. "What's he saying, Tom?"

"Oh, shut up, Midge," I said. I knew what would happen next, but nothing I could do would stop it.

The boys, one by one, gave their share to Weedle. If they believed he was only a snow smugger, it made no difference. Perhaps they thought it was only an insult I'd shouted at him. Without a doubt, Weedle was still the king of his kingdom, and the others paid their share. Oten did, and Midgely did, and Carrots and the rest. Then *my* turn came around. "Pay up," said Weedle.

Penny laughed. "Pay *you*! He ain't giving you *noffink*!" He grinned a frightful grin that vanished as I passed along my bowl. "What's they done to you?" he asked. "You was never cowed and womble-cropped."

It was his turn next. The smallest at the table, a twisted cripple of a boy, he alone stood up to Weedle. "Go hang yourself," he said. "You thick-wit."

Every boy drew his breath. But Benjamin Penny just picked up his spoon and began to eat. The sounds that came from him were the snuffles and grunts of a piggery. He was loathesome but brave. He spared not a glance for Weedle.

Penny stayed by my side every minute. All through the morning he was there, wedging himself between Midgely and me. "Shove off!" he told Midge. "Want a nosebender?"

I felt so sorry for Midgely. He never said a word, but always

moved aside when Penny came snuffling and slouching between us. He looked sad, and my heart went out to him. I made
certain that I was beside him at the noontime meal, and when
Penny tried to worm in, I told him, "Go away!"

"But, Smashy," cried Penny.

"Are you stupid?" I said. "Can't you see I'm not him? I
never was."

"You've forgot. It was that crack on the head, Smashy."
He clawed at my clothes. "Look here. I'll show you."

I pushed him aside. I nearly sent him flying backward
from the bench, but up he got again. Weedle watched it all
with his scar twitching. He was fit to kill, but what did it matter? That night I would be rid of him forever.

The ship's bell tolled the half hours, through the longest
day I'd spent on the hulk. When it rang us up from our work,
the wind was rising again, the rain beating on the deck. I
threw down my pieces of cloth, the last bits of wretched
cloth that I would ever have to see. I rose from the bench.

But a guard pushed me back. His cane smacked across
my shoulders, and I gasped at the shock.

There was a needle missing from our table. With the
benches full of thieves and pickpockets, it could have been
taken by anyone at all. I hoped it was Midgely, but he only
looked at me with a frown and a shrug. Then the cane battered one of us, and then another, each of us in turn. Oten
Acres folded up and wept, and Penny shrieked each time the
cane whacked his twisted bones. All of us were marked for
punishment in the morning.

The thought that I would be gone by then gave me a
calmness that seemed to puzzle Weedle as much as it pleased
Benjamin Penny, who must have seen a glimpse of his old
Smasher. A glimpse, though, was all it was. When he saw me
get up and follow the noseys to chapel, he gasped.

"You? To *chapel?*" he asked. "Who is it what ruined you, Smashy?"

For the first time, Midgely asked to go with me. He pulled at my sleeves, and he wept when I pushed him away. "Please take me, Tom," he begged.

It was too much for me. "Shut up," I told him. "You're a pest, Midgely. I don't even like you sometimes."

I went alone. I knelt beside my closed panel, intending to pray with everyone else. But my thoughts strayed to London, to the lonely churchyard where my diamond lay, and then to Mr. Goodfellow. I imagined the look on his face when I met him again.

I felt the ship touch the bottom, then roll away and touch again. The chaplain squinted at his Bible, his wisps of hair shining like a halo in the lamplight. I hoped he wouldn't hate me when he learned that I'd been tunneling from his chapel. I wished I could say goodbye. But I left in silence with the others, feeling all atingle with excitement and dread. I would soon be out on the marshes, and the thought of that pleased me very much. But I would soon be alone, and the thought of *that* disturbed me.

I didn't like to admit it, but I would miss little Midgely. It would be a hard thing to leave him in the marshes and hurry on without him. But his usefulness was over now. I would find a place for him to hide, and tell him, "Now wait here while I look ahead. Wait until I call." I wondered how long he would lie there before he realized I would never call.

Selfish, I told myself. Yes, it was so. But if the hulk had taught me anything, it was that I had to look out for myself. Dog eat dog, that was the rule.

I followed in the line from the chapel to the place where I always sat with Midgely. I heard the voices, the whispers, and saw the little crowd gathered in the corner. And I knew right away that something was terribly wrong.

Midgely was curled into a tight ball, rocking himself on the tilted deck. "Where's Tom?" he was saying. "Where's Tom Tin?"

I rushed to his side. Around us stood the boys, Weedle on my left, Penny on my right.

"Help me, Tom," said Midge.

I fell beside him; I held him. His small hands groped toward me. His eyes were closed, and covered with blood—with blood and more. Tears and pus and a red-stained jelly glued his eyelids shut.

"It hurts, Tom," he said. "It hurts like the devil, it does."

I tried to wipe away the blood and wetness. His eyes felt squishy, soft as rotted fruit. Benjamin Penny leaned over my shoulder, breathing fast, hoarse breaths. He shuddered as I lifted the lids of Midgely's eyes.

They were punctured, those eyes. They were collapsing, dribbling their fluid through jagged holes. I knew in a flash why the needle had been stolen from our table.

"I didn't cry out," said Midge. "Not a sound. I was a meek, Tom." His hands pressed at my chest like a cat's paws. "You would have been proud of me."

Just behind him, his hands at his sides, Weedle was standing and watching. On his face was the same dark look he always wore, twisted by his scar into a smile of wicked pleasure.

I leapt at him. I knew exactly what I was doing, and just what I was giving up to do it. If it meant I would spend seven years on the hulk, it didn't matter at all right then. I sprang up, over Midgely and across the floor, through the ring of boys. I grabbed Weedle by the throat.

He staggered back; I pressed toward him. I trampled on

142

his irons and pushed again, and down we went, slamming to the floor. I put all my weight on his neck, and drove his head against the wood. I heard him gasp and choke. His feet kicked in a rattle of chains; his fists bashed at my ribs. But I didn't let go. I would never let go, I thought.

Poor Midge called out, "Tom! Oh, Tom, what are you doing?"

A rage throbbed in my head. My blood roared like heavy surf, and my breath came in great walloping grunts. As though from very far away, I heard Benjamin Penny laugh. "There's the old Smashy," he cried. "It *is* you; it's you after all. Kill him, Smashy. Kill him!"

It was just what I wanted to do. I wanted it with all my heart. But the commotion brought a guard, and at the sound of his boots thumping along the deck, the boys pulled us apart. It took every boy in the ward to pry me away, and still I struggled against them.

Penny cackled as Weedle went scuttling back to the wall. "Cooked his goose!" he cried. "You did it, Smashy!"

The hot rush in my head turned to a spreading chill. Yes, I had done it. I had nearly throttled the life from a boy. I was glad—almost proud—that I had at last stood up for myself and for Midgely, but what I had done left me cold. I saw then that I was as savage as any other, no better than the worst of them. The Smasher and I were one and the same.

When the guards arrived, Weedle was sobbing in the corner. He raised a hand and pointed at me. "It was him," he said. "He's the one what did it." Right there and then I was hauled off to the Overseer, up through the rain and wind.

The ship was firmly on the bottom, leaning at an angle that made the guards seem strangely out of balance as they dragged and pushed me along. With the rain stinging in my eyes I peered off at the marshes, where the water broke in a pale line of white surf. The muddy shore had never seemed closer.

The Overseer didn't bother to open his door. He only shouted through it, "What's his name? What's he done?"

"It's Tom Tin, sir," said the guard. "He was fighting."

I heard the Overseer grunt. "You can cage a beast, but you can't make him tame," he said. "Mark him for punishment in the morning." My heart rose for a moment, then sank again when he added, "And double his irons tonight."

It looked like miles of chains that the negro blacksmith came dragging down the deck. He fastened them on, and I staggered below with nearly fifty pounds of metal on my legs. I couldn't even climb into my hammock. Instead, I lay on the hard wood of the deck as the guards locked us down. Then I struggled to my feet and shook Midgely.

"Tom?" he asked, his hands reaching up. I took them, and held them. I said, "It's time."

"I can't see," he said. "Leave me, Tom, and go on your own."

I had gotten exactly what I wished. It was as though he had been blinded only because I'd hoped to be rid of him. And now I couldn't do it. "I'm taking you with me," I said. "I won't leave you behind."

He smiled. "I don't mind, Tom. I know you didn't want me along." His voice sounded more childlike, more slurred than ever. "Nobody doesh, Tom. Nobody ever wantsh me."

I was ashamed. "That's nonsense, Midge," I said.

"No, it ain't." He shook his head. "Me dad didn't want me, Tom. He left me. Me mam turned me out. I don't mind anymore; it's all right."

"I'll carry you," I said, and meant it. Even dragging fifty pounds of metal, I would carry him and his irons too, all the way to London. "Now come on, Midge. I'll help you."

144

His eyes were such a mess that I couldn't tell, in the gloom of the ship, if they were open or closed. I scooped him from his hammock and brought him to the deck, and he held on to my neck like a baby. "Blesh you, Tom," he said.

From Weedle we had nothing to fear. He was sobbing in his hammock, and even his shabby gang left him alone. My only worry was Benjamin Penny. Below the swaying canvas he was already coming toward us with his scuttling, monkey-like gait. With hand and hip, he lurched and slid across the deck.

"Who's that?" asked Midgely.

"Only Penny," said I.

"No! Tell him he can't," said Midge. "I don't want him with us." He tugged at my shirt. "Send him away."

Penny said nearly the same thing of Midge when he rattled up to my side. "Where you going wiff *him*?" he asked. "It's always me and you, Smashy."

Midgely didn't argue, but his hands kneaded and pressed. A nasty little plan formed in my mind, the sort of thing I imagined the Smasher might have dreamed up. "We're all going," I said in a whisper. "All of us together."

Oten Acres was waiting by the edge of the hammocks. Our shirts wrapped around our chains, the four of us trekked through the ship. Midgely and I went hand in hand, but blind or not, he knew the way as well as I.

In the chapel I uncovered the hole; I threw the panel aside. Oten took up our sad lot of tools and went at the wood with his thinned arms. I waited for a wall of water to come bursting in upon us.

Oten held the spike like a chisel. He drove it against the wood a hundred times before it went right through. He pierced the plank, and only air came in. Cool and fresh, it smelled of trees, of mud, of freedom, in a way. The farm boy widened the hole. He put his face to the jagged edge he'd made and breathed deeply for a moment. Then he drew back with his hair wet from the rain. He was smiling. "Thank you, Tom," he said.

He ripped through the wood, smashing the planks. When the hole was wide enough he moved aside to let me look.

The river was no more than a foot from the edge of the hole. Distant waves leapt in the wind, but here the river was sheltered. I couldn't see the marshes, but I heard the surf squishing at their edge, and the snicker and scythe of the long-bladed grass bending in the wind.

"Are there lights? Are there sentries?" asked Midge.

"Nothing," said I. "It's like looking into a kettle."

I used one of the canes to test the river's depth. I leaned from the hole, reaching far into the water, but felt no bottom.

The ship was leaning steeply now. Once we dropped clear we could never come back. It was on to the marshes or drown. I gave the other cane to Midgely.

"Penny goes first," I said.

Penny was pleased, but Midge not at all. "He didn't do no digging. Why does *he* go first?" he said.

" 'Cause he knows how I can swim," said Penny. "Like a fish, ain't I, Smashy?"

"Yes," I lied. "That's right." I even gave him a pat on his twisted shoulder as I thought how nasty and cunning I was. If Benjamin Penny made it to shore, then all of us could. And if he didn't, well. . . . I would rather lose him than Oten, and I would never let Midgely go first.

Penny pulled himself to the hole. "See you in London, Smashy," he said. And out he went feetfirst. For a moment he hung by his fingers as the current pulled him away. Then the webs of skin spread open, and down he sank.

I flew to the hole and saw his hands disappearing into

that frightful darkness. I imagined him falling to the bottom, then crawling toward the marshes—would he know which way it was? I neither saw nor heard him reach the shore.

Oten was next. He put his broad shoulders through the hole and didn't wait another instant. Headfirst he dove to the river, his feet dragging across the floor. But his irons jammed against the planks, leaving him dangling there with the water churning in his struggle. I picked up his chains, his ankles, and heaved him out.

Only Midgely was left with me then. His eyes were still pasted shut, but he groped his way to the hole, and out from the ship, until he hung from the edge as Penny had done. With one hand he gripped the wood, and with the other he took the hollow canes. He even found a way to help me out, though the water made him gasp and shudder. He tucked the canes in his shirt, freeing his hand to pull at my irons, to drag them through the hole.

Cold as ice, the river swallowed my feet, my legs, my waist, and my chest. The rain soaked the rest of me; the irons dragged me down. I held on to the ship and gazed up its side, unwilling to let go. I was certain that I would plummet straight to my death, that my cane wouldn't reach the surface, that the currents would tear me away from Midge.

I could feel him shaking. Already my feet were numb from the cold, and I knew we could wait no longer. Midgely passed me one of the canes. I put the end in my mouth, and he did the same with his. We held hands, my fingers enclosing his whole fist, and a memory of my sister came clearly to my mind; her hand had been just the same size.

"Don't let me go," said Midge.

nineteen
WITH MIDGELY IN THE MARSHES

We dropped into the river. Water slammed at my ears as it closed above my head. I felt myself falling. The cane buoyed up, then sprang from my lips and shot toward the surface. Soon my chains settled on the bottom.

In desperation, I tried to run, to haul myself somehow to the surface. But the irons held my feet, and Midgely held my hand, and I felt panic overwhelm me. I was living all the nightmares I'd ever had of the sea, of drowning. Yet the worst of them had been nothing compared to the fear I felt now.

I bent my knees and sprang forward. I hopped across the riverbed, once and twice, until my swollen lungs felt as though they'd burst. I tried to reach the surface, but Midgely pulled me down. He was dragging me to my doom, I thought, until my flailing hand found the stones on the river bottom. Then I pulled at one and inched along, and my breath exploded in a great bubble. My chest pulsed and heaved as I pulled myself forward. I found a chain and, in my panic, let go of Midge to grab it.

I drew up my legs and reached higher. In my breathlessness I couldn't make sense of what came into my hands. It moved wherever I touched it, swaying and sinking. Soft in places, hard in others, it felt like a great sea plant covered in loose and leafy skin. I hauled myself up, pushing the thing down until my head broke the surface. I gasped deep breaths.

The ship was only yards away, an enormous wall of wood. A lamp was burning above the deck, swinging in a globe of golden, shining rain. The marshes were even closer. I could see Midgely sprawled at their edge, his knees and feet in the water, his hands grabbing at the grass.

Then I saw what held me up. The thick tendrils were arms and fingers, the fronds a person's hair. Oten Acres, the poor farmer's boy, floated in the river, moored by his chains. His arms weaved round and over each other, as though he swam in the current.

I nearly shouted in my horror. But I gathered my wits and held on, and his head lolled in the current, tipping sideways. I saw his face below the surface. It wore a look of pleasure, of peace and contentment. The mouth was smiling, the eyes closed, and I could see that Oten—for a moment, at least— had found his freedom.

I rested as I held him. Then I hopped and crawled and dragged myself up from the river to Midgely's side. He cried out when I touched him, and sobbed at the sound of my voice. "I thought I'd lost you, Tom," he said.

There was no sign of Benjamin Penny, and we spared him no thought. We squirmed through the mud, a dozen yards into the grasses, then stopped in exhaustion. There, sodden and frozen, we huddled together as the wind swept the blades of grass, as the rain pelted our faces.

The morning came slowly. We smelled the smoke from the ship's cooking fire, then heard the bell across the water. Soon came the tramping feet and the irons ringing, the shouts of the guards as they hurried the boys. In our nest in the marshes, I wondered if Midgely felt the same as I, if he wished himself back on the ship just then. My teeth were chattering, my hands shaking, but as miserable as I was, Midgely must have been worse. His eyes looked like old, half-rotten potatoes—shrunken and soft. A tarry mass glued them shut.

I washed them for him, scooping water from the ground. I wet his eyes as gently as I could, then pried them open. Midgely winced but never cried. "I can see you, Tom," he said. "You're just a smudge, Tom. All I see is smudges."

"You'll get better," I said, though I didn't believe it. His eyes were gray and lifeless.

I hated to make him get up and move along. But I was eager to make distance from the ship, and couldn't wait for Midge to rest. Even as I nudged him, a great commotion rose on the hulk, and the air filled with shouts. Almost instantly came the shocking bang of a cannon. The blast thudded in my ears.

"That's the signal," said Midgely. "Now the soldiers will come."

"We have to get moving," I told him.

"Ain't we going to hide right here?" he asked. "Ain't that your plan?"

It was what I had told him we would do. I had hoped he would dig himself into the mud, where the soldiers would find him right away. Anything that slowed the soldiers down would help me get away. *That* had been my plan.

"I've had a change of heart," I said. "Come on, Midge."

My idea that I could stroll away through fields of grass

150

seemed pathetic now. We had to slither and crawl, dragging more weight in irons than Midgely weighed himself. We found ourselves stuck in the gummy mud, and the soldiers coming already. Between tufts of grass I saw their boats scudding down the river from the naval yard. Three abreast, five more behind, they came in puffs of spray and flashing oars.

"Hurry, Midge," I said.

Through the grass and through the rain, I dragged myself and Midgely too. I hauled him over hummocks, into puddles, round clusters of grass too thick to go through. He shivered and panted. "It ain't no use," he said. "Go on by yourself." But I told him more lies; they came easily now. I told him there were trees ahead, a place to shelter, though all I really saw was grass and more grass. It stretched on forever, it seemed.

We hadn't gone very far when the soldiers landed. I could still see the masts of the *Lachesis,* and I heard very plainly the long, drumming rattle as the soldiers fixed their bayonets. I heard the scratchy sizzle as they waded through the grass behind us. "Hurry, Midge," I said.

We crawled like lizards, with our bellies in the mud. When Midge could go no farther, I had him climb on my back and I carried him along. The soldiers came steadily, and the cannon boomed from the ship, and my hands were cut raw by the grasses. I pulled and pushed us along, snaking through the hollows. I thought we would never get out of the marsh. But, finally, I swept the rushes aside and saw we had come to the edge.

"Why have you stopped?" asked Midgely, clinging to my back. I could feel him shaking with the cold, and hear the chatter of his teeth. "What do you see?" he said.

I didn't want to tell him. The marsh lay behind us, yet what stretched ahead was worse. Right before me, on either side, flowed water deep and gray. It churned in a current even stronger than the one that tugged at the *Lachesis*. Plumed with whitecaps, dotted with fishermen's boats, it was wider than London's grandest streets.

"What's the matter, Tom?" asked Midgely.

"Oh, Midge, we're on an island."

I wasn't sure if he laughed or sobbed. Perhaps the sound he made was a bit of both. "Well, we tried, Tom," he said.

It might have been a kindness to him if I had stood up and waved my arms to bring the soldiers. It was surely what he wanted me to do. But I had gone too far to give up.

Out on the river the fishermen's boats rolled and pitched. Only one was working, and it was tearing toward us, a man in the middle rowing like the devil straight against the wind. It plunged through clouds of spray; the oars shed streams of water. Heaped around the rower was a net, and sitting on the top of it was a small figure wrapped in oilskins.

Perhaps I only saw what I cared to see. But a hope formed in my mind, and then a certainty, that this fellow was coming to save me. I imagined that he'd spent his whole life fishing with his son in the foul shadow of the hulk, that he'd come to loathe it, to teach his son to fear it. Perhaps he had waited years for the chance to help a boy escape.

"Stay here," I told Midge. "Lie low and wait."

I crawled from the grass to the mud of the bank, then got to my knees and waved both arms. The child—it was surely a child balanced high on the net—pointed toward me. The fisherman rowed even harder, driving into the waves until the spray hurled up and enveloped all three—the boat, the man, and the child.

I stood up for an instant. The soldiers were coming, still far across the marsh, but coming shoulder to shoulder in a line that stretched clear across the island. Their red shoulders, their tall black hats, rose above the grasses.

The boat came ashore. Up sprang the fisherman, dropping his oars. He leapt into water up to his knees, grabbed the boat, and hauled it in. Waves broke on its side and pushed it around. Then the child stood up—but not a child at all. Wrapped in oilskins was a wizened old woman, a shrunken hag who must have had the eyes of a hawk.

"It *is* him," she cried. "Didn't I say 'That's Jacob there?' "

"That you did." The fisherman pushed back the big, broad hat he wore. "Saints preserve me! It's him right enough."

"Not Jacob, sir," I said. "I'm Tom."

The old woman cackled. "Well, Jacob you were born. Didn't I name you that myself? Didn't I haul you from the water, you as blue as blazes, with the devil already inside you?"

"No," I said. "I—"

"That she did." The fisherman loosened his coat, and the wind tore it off. He swirled it around and over my shoulders, like a great ragged bird covering me with an enormous wing. "So this is where you've come to, Jacob. Out in the marshes, fleeing from the hulks."

I had no doubt who Jacob was. It seemed that wherever I went, however I ran, my dead twin would come shambling after. He had pursued me all the way from London, and bit by bit I was coming to know him. Now he had a name.

"Please listen," I said. "I live in London, in Camden now, and—"

"Weren't you born below the Beacon Hill?" The woman stood in the wind, and it pulled at her clothes as she pointed across the marsh. "Right there? On a dark night, in a howl of wind, in the storms of harvest time?"

She knew more than was natural. My father's village had

been just below that hill. I had been born there in November.
"But—"

"Didn't your mother put you in the river? Straight in the river like a cat to be drowned, when she saw the devil inside you?"

"No!" I shook my head.

"Didn't I haul you out from the fishes myself? Didn't we care for you like our own, until the law took you off at the age of six? Oh, you were a smart little man at six, Jacob boy, striking the fear of God into all of us."

The fisherman crossed himself. Then he turned his head toward the marshes, and with a startled cry he asked, "Who's that?"

It was Midgely, half hidden in the grass. Caked in black, his dead eyes staring, he looked more like a lizard than a boy. I told him, "Come out," and he blundered from the marsh on his hands and knees. The sight of him would have roused pity in anyone else, but the fisherman quickly crossed himself again.

"Tom?" bleated Midgely. "Where are you, Tom?"

I went to his side, and the old woman came too. She stamped through the water, through the mud, rushing toward us. For one mad moment I thought she would say she knew *Midgely* too, by some other name and some wild story. But suddenly she seemed to soften. She laid her coat over Midgely. "Poor wee thing," she said.

The soldiers were running. Pale light gleamed on their buttons and badges. Their red coats rippled.

"Quickly, Isaac," said the woman. "Put the boys in the boat."

The fisherman did what he was told. He picked up Midgely, chains and all, and set him atop the net. I hobbled toward him, and he came back for me. He gathered me up as easily as he'd taken Midge. Then the woman got in, and the man shoved the boat from the mud, and soon we were tossing across the water.

"Don't you move now, Jacob boy," said the woman. "Don't you move a muscle." She arranged the oilskins on top of us, hiding our heads and feet. "Didn't I say it would be a lucky morning?" she asked the fisherman.

"That you did." Spray flew up and pelted against the cloth.

"Where will you take us?" I asked.

"Home," said the woman. "Now lie still, Jacob boy, and not another word."

I wondered where they lived. It might be the same little village where I had been born; it was bound to be nearby. I would meet people who had known my father. Surely there would be someone to help me.

I lay covered in the oilskins, atop the hard coils and corks that smelled of fish. Slowly I warmed, my shivers becoming less violent. But along with my warmth came the seasickness. The slamming of the boat, its dizzying rolls and lurches, wrapped my innards into their old, familiar knots. For once, though, I didn't mind. It was worth all the wooziness and all the trembles—and more—to be on my way to London.

Rain pattered on the heavy cloth, and now and then a burst of spray ran rivers down its edges. Midgely's little hand found mine, and I held it. I was frightened and sick, but happy as could be.

Then the fisherman stopped his rowing.

The old woman pulled away the oilskins, and my heart fell when I saw what she had meant by "home."

twenty

A LONELY CHRISTMAS

Midgely came out from the old woman's coat like a turtle. His head and hands appeared. "Where are we?" he asked.

I couldn't bring myself to tell him. We were back at the hulk, at the *Lachesis*. The boat plunged at the foot of the steps, on waves that rolled over the landing, over the boots of soldiers and guards. It surged up the steps to the feet of the Overseer.

"Haul them out," he said. "Put them in the black hole."

We were shifted like baggage, out of the boat and up to the deck. The fisherman's woman was shrieking at the Overseer. At the top of her voice she demanded a reward for delivering us home.

The guards locked us into the black hole, each into our own narrow space. It was hard enough for *me* to be put in there, but for Midge it was almost torture. He cried out, "I can't see!" And then, "Are you there, Tom?" And I answered him, "Yes. Oh, Midge, I'm so sorry."

For days and days we were kept in the black hole. I could neither stretch out on the floor nor stand beneath the ceiling. I had to curl like a bug, or crook myself against the curve of the wall. There was no day and no night, nothing but a never-ending darkness. Even the quaver of the ship's bell didn't reach me down there. Time meant nothing.

If it weren't for Midgely, the black hole might have made me a drooling, mumbling lunatic. It was my worry for *him,* at first, that set me talking nonstop. But soon I needed the sound of his voice, and thought I might go moony without it. "Tell me about your islands," I said. "Tell me about the one with the village." Tell me of this one, I would say; tell me of that one. And Midge went on and on, sometimes quoting whole paragraphs straight from the book. I learned the names of the islands, their harbors and villages.

I began to see them and smell them, and when I wasn't tramping across those islands with Midge, I was dreaming myself upon them. Deep in dark jungles I would come across my father, and we would wander down winding trails to beaches of sand so bright in the sun that my eyes ached from the gleam.

To wake from that to utter blackness was almost too much sometimes. As often as not, I would hear Midgely weeping, calling for me. "I'm here," I'd say, and off we'd go again.

When at last we were let out, I couldn't stand up. It was as though my legs had forgotten how to hold me. My brain, so used to seeing lush islands, couldn't make sense of the wooden walls and wooden decks.

Two guards dragged me along, and another dragged Midgely. The workday had just ended, and the convicts were gathering for their meal. They watched us come in, our chains rumbling, and watched us being slumped in our places. Midgely had to grope for the edge of the table, though his eyes were open. They looked gray and cheesy now, like old half-rotted hardboiled eggs.

He whispered at me. "Are they here, Tom? Oten and that horrible boy, are they back?"

"No," I said. I had almost forgotten that Oten Acres wouldn't be there—*couldn't* be there ever again. I remembered his drowned body in the river, but it seemed so very long ago. And Benjamin Penny? What had happened to him?

Weedle was in his place at the head of the table. The bruises I had given him were still not completely healed. His eyes were as dark as ever, his twisted scar as evil-looking, yet there was something different in his manner.

"Eleven days," he said.

I didn't understand. Beside me, Midgely squirmed. "Eleven days," he echoed, then looked at me and grinned. He was already his old self. "Holy jumping mother of Moses, Tom. That's more than anyone ever."

"Was it that long?" I asked. I could hardly believe it. Christmas had passed. The whole year had ended and a new one begun.

Weedle touched his tongue to his lips. He was collecting his shares from the boys, and it was nearly my turn. Perhaps he saw in my eyes that I wouldn't give up so much as a spoonful. Perhaps he never meant to ask. But he passed over Midge and me, and told the redheaded Carrots, "Give a share to *him*. To Smasher there." He even tried to smile at me. "Bygones, eh, Smashy? Forgive and forget?"

He was scared of me now; it was fear in his eyes. Like any bully, Weedle was afraid of being beaten twice.

"Don't call me that," I said. "Don't call me Smashy."

"Sure, Tom." He nodded and twitched, then snapped at the boy. "Hurry up, Carrots. Give him your share."

"No," I said. "Eat your own. Everyone; eat your own."

That was the end of sharing. In our little kingdom in a filthy ship, a little king had toppled. I saw such a wretched look on Weedle's face that I nearly pitied him. He had lost his treasured throne, and most of his faithful army. Inside, he must have boiled with rage at what I had done to him. But outwardly, he was now—in Midgely's words—a meek. He was the meekest of the meek, bobbing up when I came near, as though ready to scurry away.

There was no chapel that evening; the kindly old chaplain was gone. Carrots said he'd been taken away to be shot, but I didn't really believe it. Carrots seemed to know everything and nothing all at once. So instead of chapel, I spent my time with Midgely's book. We sat in our same old place, but everything else was different. No longer could Midgely see the pictures He touched his fingers to the pages, as though to feel the image in the ink. "Oh, Tom," he said. "I wish I had one more day to look at them."

I didn't read a single word. All Midgely wanted was for me to describe the pictures—every detail, every line. But I couldn't see in the smudges what he wanted me to see, and it was a sad hour for the both of us. I was glad when the time ended, and the ship began to lock down for the night. In my doubled irons, I felt too weak to walk on deck. I looked at Weedle, told him, "Fetch my hammock," and saw him nod.

"Sure, Tom," he cried.

"Midgely's too," I said.

Up he went and down he came, then held out the bundles toward me. I had only to look toward the grated window to set him nodding again. "Sure, Tom," said he. "I'll hang them there. No fear."

I spent the night as Oten had spent his—gazing out at black water, at things I couldn't see. I dreaded the additional punishment that would surely come in the morning. I feared the cat-o'-nine-tails.

It was still dark when Weedle carried my hammock away. Weedle fetched my breakfast, and even washed my bowl. At ten o'clock he looked at me in worry, as though I meant to send him in my place to see the Overseer.

I went up with Midgely. We crossed the deck below a gray sky of torn clouds, with the sun behind them like a smear of mustard, and were left to wait at the Overseer's door. On the far side of the river, a boat was drawn up on the beach, its rowers sitting like men at a picnic. In the marsh above them, a boy was being buried. By the size of the bundle that was all he'd become, it must have been Oten Acres. Wrapped in brown cloth, he was heaved into the ground with only a guard and a gravedigger for mourners.

I wondered if Worms would get him, if old Worms would come riding out with his three-legged horse and bear Oten away, at last, to the city he had hoped to see. *"I been out to Woolwich and the Medway now and then to fetch the ones from the ships,"* Worms had told me.

I looked away, down the river toward the distant trees. A ship was working around the bend, its white sails fluttering. As much as I hated the sea, and anything that moved upon it, the sight of that ship gliding over the water was a picture of freedom itself. Three masts soared up from the marsh, dazzling sails moving along above the grass like the banners of a marching army. Then the dark hull emerged, growing long and graceful, bearing the towers of white canvas.

To my surprise, Midgely turned toward it. "Is there a ship coming, Tom?" he asked.

"Can you see it?" I said.

"I can *hear* it," he said. "I can hear the wind in the sails." He tugged my arm. "How many masts has she got? Topgallants, Tom? Royals? Has she got skysails, Tom? Can you count the yards?"

"Count the *what*?" I said. He had taught me a bit about ships, but nothing like that. I asked him, "What are yards?"

"Spars, Tom." Then he sighed and said, "Them sideways sticks what holds the sails."

It pained him, I saw, to put it like that. But I counted them off, six on each mast, and he whistled. "Holy jumping mother of Moses. She's a ship, Tom. A real ship."

I didn't know then that not every ship was a ship. But as Midgely rubbed his eyes and stared toward it, I wished he could see more clearly. There was beauty and grace in that thing.

"You know why she's here?" said Midge. "She's come to take us to Australia. Sure as eggs, we'll be transported."

His words robbed the ship of its beauty. They turned it to a lurking horror, a black beast creeping up the river.

"All's Bob now," said Midge. "No more hulk. No more guards and nobs and Weedles. Yes, all's Bob now."

"It will be just the same somewhere else," I said.

"Oh, no," said he. "It will have to be a better place where we're going."

The Overseer called us in. He sat in his wooden armchair, dressed in white. His shirt was fine and ruffled, his breeches and stockings tight as skin. He looked like a fat poodle close-cut round the legs and wooly at the head. He frowned at Midgely. "What's wrong with your eyes?" he said.

"It was an accident, sir," said Midge. "I fell on a needle."

"Twice on the same needle?"

Midgely nodded. "It was an accident, sir."

161

The Overseer leaned toward him, then away in disgust. "This accident, boy. Tell me his name."

"Please, sir, it was just an accident." Midgely bit his lip. "And Tom here, sir, he don't know his name neither."

"I see. You boys can pick a pocket and cut a throat, but never tell a tale. Is that it?" The Overseer's hands came together on the bulge of his belly. "You caused me a great deal of trouble. I shall have to enter all this in the Occurrence Book. One boy dead and another missing, and a ruddy big hole in my ship. What have you to say for yourselves?"

Midge looked down at the deck, a study in remorse. It was surely what the Overseer wanted. He would be pleased by that, delighted if we begged for mercy. But I found myself annoyed by his foppish clothes, incensed by the finery of a cabin so near to our misery. Not minding what punishment he gave me, I squared my shoulders and said, "I'm sorry Oten died. He was a friend of mine, and I liked him. But he was dying already, because your ship was killing him, and I gave him a bit of hope, and I'm proud of that."

Midgely trembled, and the Overseer looked astonished. His fingers ran up through the ruffles on his shirt, up to his chin. "Why, you're full of guts, aren't you, boy? A frumper, you are," he said. "I could give you a flogging for an outburst like that. But there's worse in store for you, my boy."

twenty-one
BEYOND THE SEAS

The Overseer wetted his lips. He stretched his fat legs, and the chair creaked below him like the timbers of the ship. He touched the papers on his table. "I've made my lists," he said. "You were recommended for liberty, Tom. Do you know that? The chaplain suggested I set you free."

He looked straight into my eyes. "Well, you're being transported now. The pair of you are. We'll see what a spell in Australia does to that spirit of yours."

I managed to swallow the fear that was choking my throat. The Overseer stared at me, and I stared right back. Then he turned away to his papers, his fat lips set in a pout. "That is all," he said.

The distant ship had anchored when we came out. It sat right in the bend of the river, with men working way up on Midgely's blessed sticks. If I had to go to Australia, at least I was glad it was to be in something as large as that, as solid as an island. Then I remembered the picture in Midgely's book, *Summer off the Cape,* where the water had looked like a range of snowy mountains. I tried to put that ship into the drawing, and frightened myself half to death.

Midgely sang. Barely above his breath, he launched into a sea song, a ditty of sailors and hauling on ropes. I imagined he had sung it in his home, in his dingy parlor, or had had it sung *to* him by the sailors who had called on his mother. In his creaky child's voice, hardly more than a whisper, he warbled away. "We're bound for the Rio," he sang. "And away, Rio! Aye, Rio!"

I gave him a shove and told him to stop. "You don't know where the Rio is," I said.

"I do," said he. "It's in the Americas, Tom."

"And we're going the other way," I told him.

"No, we ain't!" he cried. "We go all the way across the ocean, and all the way back. That'sh how it worksh, Tom. That'sh the windsh for you."

He sang again. He sang that song as we worked, sang it as we ate, as we tramped around the deck. He was still singing when we settled down in the evening, below the grating where Weedle had sat before. The cold night's air blew across us, plucking at the lamp flames, and in flickering shadows the boys played at their pitch-button game.

"How long will it take to get to Australia?" I asked.

"Oh, a hundred days," said Midge, as though it were nothing. "Maybe a hundred and fifty."

"Five months?" I groaned. It didn't seem possible. How could a ship set out from land and not touch it again for nearly *half a year*?

"Sometimes it's longer," said Midge quite cheerfully. "In the First Fleet, the *Sirius* took two hundred and sixty days to get to Australia. Think of it, Tom." His voice squeaked. "Two hundred and shixshty days!"

"Shut up!" I told him.

He drew away with a little gasp. I saw the hurt look on his face, and was instantly sorry. When I reached toward him he cringed at what must have seemed like a blurred fist coming at him.

"Midge," I said. "The truth is . . ." It was hard to admit. The boys were arguing at their button game, all standing now, suddenly close to blows. I leaned toward Midgely and said in a whisper, "I'm a little afraid of the sea."

"Afraid of the sea?" he echoed too loudly. "The son of Redman Tin? Your blood's salt water, Tom."

"Well, it feels like ice," I said.

"We was born for the sea. Captains' boys and all." There was a smile on his lips, and it made his dead eyes especially strange. "It's like no matter what we did, we would someday go to sea."

Perhaps he was right. My mother had done all she could to shield me from the sea. She'd hidden me from it, as though she'd feared that Neptune himself might have stolen me away like a Gypsy or a chimney sweep. She had raised me to love the city and hate the sea, and she'd taught me so well that I'd screamed and kicked on a summer day when my father tried to put me into a paddling boat on Regent's Pond. But one turn of fate after another had seen to it that I would follow my father in his watery ways.

"It's queer, though, ain't it?" said Midge. "You'll look straight in the face at what fears you. I'll get what I want, but I won't see a thing." He turned his shoulders and tipped up his head. "Promise you'll be my eyes? You can tell me what it's like, the waves and the albatrosses and all. I wanted so much to see an albatross. Promise me that?"

165

"I will." I patted his hand, feeling ashamed. If a frail blind boy wasn't frightened, then why was I?

On the Sabbath that week I didn't pray for my deliverance. I knelt in my chains and asked only for courage.

The next morning we were off on our way. Sixteen boys were sorted out for transportation, Weedle and Carrots among them. Four boats came to fetch us, nuzzling up to the side of the ship like piglets to a filthy sow. Then the dawn broke in glorious colors, and the Overseer came to stand on his high deck. Above us, against the crimson and the yellow, he might have been the figure in a stained-glass window high in a great cathedral.

"Lest any of you think that Fate is cruel, remember this," said he. "You had a fair start."

He looked at us for so long that I thought it was all he had to say. Then the wind lifted his hair like a puff of smoke, and plucked at the ruffles of his shirt. His voice boomed out. "Don't think that England has turned her back on you, boys. She expects you to return as men one day. Remember always that you are British. God save the King!"

He got no answering shout, no huzza from us. We closed tightly together as the guards came to move us off. They marched us to the landing and into the boats, and I sat with Midgely in the stern of one, with a pair of men to row us. Down the river we went, the wind behind us, past the marshes and the castle. I glanced back at the hulk and saw it sitting steady in the water, the British flag streaming. Nothing in the world could have looked more awful and evil. With a shudder I turned to face the front, looking past the rowers to the Beacon Hill rising to its flat top. The dark ship was below it, and in the river's bend grew a floating forest of masts and sideways sticks.

The waves tipped us up, tipped us down, and we sped

toward the ship. The rowers chewed big quids of tobacco that bubbled yellow from their lips. Their backs bent, their arms pulled, and to my surprise we flew right past the ship. A lone sailor on the deck pulled off his cap and cheered us on.

Midgely had his eyes closed, his hand spread atop them to shield the sunlight. I didn't tell him that we passed the ship, for I saw where we were going instead, to another just beyond it.

If ships were people, then the first would have been a dark and beautiful daughter, and this her ugly stepmother. Older and smaller, battered and bruised, it lay by itself as though out of shame. It had two masts instead of three, and not nearly as many sticks. I looked up along the rigging, past sails like wadded bedclothes, to a familiar and wretched sight.

At the top of the mast, curled by the wind, flew the Goodfellow flag. Its purples and greens, its gold crest in the middle, waggled against the sky as though Fate was thumbing her nose at me.

The ship was exactly as my father had described those of the Goodfellow fleet. *"Beggars of the sea,"* he had said. *"Not fit for rotten-row. A drowning man would sooner swim than climb aboard one."*

There was a steady thumping and a run of water, a gushing like a city fountain. I'd learned its meaning well on the *Lachesis*—and Midgely knew it too. "Why are they pumping?" he said.

He started to take his hand away, but I clapped it back in place. "Don't look," I said. "Wait till we're aboard."

"She ain't old and leaky, is she, Tom?"

"No, no. She's beautiful." I hoped to save him from his disappointment. One ship was so much like another, and his eyes so bad, that I thought he might *never* discover the truth. "Keep your eyes shut tight till I tell you," I said.

Our boat bumped against the hull, and a sailor reached down with a hooked stick to catch it. Even in our irons there wasn't much climbing to do; the deck was barely above the water.

"My, she's sleek," said Midge. "She must look like a greyhound, Tom."

"Like some sort of dog," said I.

"Shall I look now, Tom?"

"No! Not yet," I cried.

The ship was a ruin. Littered with boxes and barrels and tangles of rope, with a huge stack of wood for a cargo, it looked like a tumbled old warehouse. Paint was peeling; globs of tar lay everywhere. Midgely held on to me with one hand, his other touching the railing and the ropes. Bits of paint flurried away from the wood, and tiny strands of rope went floating off in the sun. The entire ship, I thought, would fall apart like that, shedding its little pieces all across the ocean.

Weedle clambered up from the next boat, and Carrots from the third. Dampened from spray, chilled by the winter air, we stood with our heads drawn into our collars, our breath making white mist.

Way off at the front of the ship, an old man came backward from a door. He smoked a clay pipe that puffed gray clouds, and he dragged a wicker basket on the end of a rope. He paused to hoist it over the sill, gouting smoke like a steam engine. By the clanking sounds that came from his kypsey I guessed he was the blacksmith. Too frail to carry his tools, he dragged them instead, tipping forward and back as the kypsey rocked on its rounded bottom.

Midge kept touching the ropes, up and down from one to the next. "Tom?" he said. "This ain't the right ship."

Before I could speak, he opened his eyes. I didn't know what he could see exactly, but he glanced back and forth, up and down, and his face crumpled. "A brig," he said. "Just a little brig."

His disappointment turned to anger. His face was suddenly red. "A rotten trick, Tom. That wash a rotten, rotten trick." He let go of my arm. "Why didn't you shay it wash a brig?"

"How could I?" I had only meant well, so I got angry too. "I don't even know what the devil that means. I could touch the ropes till doomsday, or walk right from the front to the back and—"

"They ain't *ropes,* Tom," said Midgely. "They're *lines.* And it ain't the front and back, it's the *bow,* Tom. The bow and the stern." He sighed through his nose. "You ain't the son of Redman Tin. That was another lie."

"Midge, no," I said. But he snatched up the slack in his chains and went hobbling to the end of the line.

The old smithy huffed his way right up to us. With watery eyes he looked into our faces, then shook his head with a deep sadness and blew half a dozen quick little puffs through his pipe.

"It's summer down under, lads," he said. "You'll be warm as toast in Van Diemen's Land."

Another puff from his pipe, a sniff from his nose, and the old man eased himself to the deck. He went to work on Midgely's irons, and a moment later—with a clang and a rattle—they fell away in a heap. "How old are you, son?" he asked. Midge said, "I'm ten," and the smithy grunted. "You're not."

"Near as spit," said Midgely. "I'll be ten in a month."

"Good Christmas!"

When four boys were free of their irons, guards led them away. I watched with a pang as Midge went off with them, over a hatch and down. I felt as though we had parted forever, and could never be friends again. When the old smithy knelt before me, he tried to jolly me out of my sadness. In a whisper he told me: "Don't fear, lad, you'll soon be at sea. Half a gale in the Channel tonight, and we'll be clear of the land by dawn. It will lift your spirits, lad, when old Neptune rocks you in his arms."

He meant well, the old fool. But a gale in the Channel, no land within sight—that wasn't a thought that cheered me. When old Neptune started rocking, it wasn't my spirits he'd lift.

My irons came away. The great weight of them—more than a third of my own—tumbled to the deck. But I felt no lighter as I trudged away in my turn, over the hatch and into a ship that made the *Lachesis* seem cheerful.

The place had been washed and scrubbed. From the open hatches came light and fresh air. But nothing could cleanse the ship of a lurking sense of misery. The very wood had soaked it up, and the ship was haunted by it. It *smelled* of misery, of sickness and suffering.

"Tom?" cried Midgely. I saw him kneeling by the wall, reaching out in his blindness like the Bartimeus in his Bible book. "Tom!" he called again. "I need you."

Weedle was cowered in a corner. "I never touched him!" he cried.

I went to Midgely; I *ran* to him. The deck down there was studded with ringbolts, some with shackles attached, some with rusted bits of chain. There were bolts in the ceiling and bolts in the walls, and where Midgely knelt there was a long snake of a chain—fully the length of the ship—lying in curls and bends.

Midgely held me, his anger gone. "Oh, Tom," he said. "She's a slaver."

twenty-two
I BATTLE WITH A GIANT

Through the day and the night we lived in that space where slaves had lain not long before. By the pattern of the ringbolts, and the scars that chains had left on the wood, I could see how the people had been packed as close as the fingers of my fist. Curled like that, front to back, they must have crossed the ocean in a solid, rippling mass.

At every moment we expected to be sorted out in the same fashion, knocked down in our places and chained to the ringbolts. Word went around that the captain of our ship was a tyrant—a madman—who would come himself to lock us into our rows. Carrots said he had seen him peering down the hatch, his eyes white with craziness, his hand gripping a bloodstained lash.

Through the evening and the night other boys arrived. By dawn of the next day there were sixty or more, and still they kept coming. There were boys from every prison in the land, boys from the north with accents so broad I couldn't understand them.

I was talking to Midge when a newcomer shouted my name. In my mind I was riding in a long canoe, paddled by savages with bones through their lips, when I heard that old cry: "Smashy! Hallo!"

"It's him, ain't it?" asked Midge.

"Yes," I said. It was Benjamin Penny.

"Keep him away, Tom. Please say you'll keep him away." He sounded quite frantic. "Go and tell him we don't want him near us. He can't come into our corner."

I didn't want him there myself. He was already scuffling toward us, and I hurried to stop him halfway. But as bad as it was to see that boy turn up again like a—well, like a bad penny, it was worse to see who came behind him. Down the ladder, rung by rung, descended the boy I'd feared the most of all I'd met. At the foot of it he turned toward me, huge and solid. Gaskin Boggis, the giant from the Darkey's gang. Stooped below the timbers, he grinned with his rotted teeth.

Penny ran in that grotesque way that was his. I tried to push him aside, but he only grabbed my hands as if he thought I was trying to embrace him. "Didn't think I'd see you again," he said. "Not when they napped me on the moor." He looked up with his eye wandering. "Smashy, they got her. They hanged the Darkey."

"Good," I said, not thinking.

"What?" cried Penny. "Somebody peached on her, Smashy."

Boggis was lumbering up beside us. "It was you," he said, pointing at me. "We know it was you."

"Don't say it," cried Penny. "Smashy ain't no snitch."

"The Smasher's dead, you diblish. I seen him," growled

Boggis. "He lay on the slab at the doctor's, the old Smasher himself. And I seen the doctor bring out his head in a hatbox and chuck it in the Thames."

"That ain't true," said Penny. "Don't let him say it, Smashy. Lay it on him now."

He shifted round behind me, as though he meant to push me right against the giant. With my elbow I shoved him back. He stumbled on a ringbolt and sprawled across the deck, and the ship was a tingling stillness as Boggis came toward me.

"Kill him, Smashy. Kill him!" Penny cried.

How I wished for all the guards of the *Lachesis* with their rope ends and their canes. But there were only the boys now, and none of them moved. Midgely huddled in the corner, sobbing my name.

A grunt came from the giant, and a deep breath that moaned through his nose. His arms swung out from his chest; his hands rolled into fists. He lumbered toward me.

I wasn't half his weight, nor two-thirds his size. I was surely smarter, and I thought I might be quicker. But his fist swung so far and so fast that I couldn't move away. With one blow he knocked me to the deck.

As I looked high at his troglodyte's head, I remembered the terror I'd felt in the Darkey's lair to see him looming above me. I remembered how I'd cowered from him, and I hated that person I'd been. Over me now came a rage more powerful than the one I had turned onto Weedle at the sight of Midgely's punctured eyes. I felt my lips draw back to bare my teeth. I felt prickles on my spine, as though hairs that weren't even there were rising into hackles. I got up and stepped forward, and Boggis moved back.

He stood in the sunlight below the hatch, as big as three boys together. His fists pulsed like huge hearts; his arms bulged enormously. They could crush me into bones and blood, but I was as blind as Midgely in my rage. Head down, I rushed the giant.

It was Walter Weedle who stopped me. He flew between us, his arms spread wide to keep us apart. In a shrill voice he cried, "Don't! He'll kill you, Gaskin. He will!"

He planted one hand on my chest and one on the giant's. "Keep away from him, Gaskin. It's him, I tell you."

Weedle whirled to face me. Before I knew it, his hand was in my collar, and my shirt was wrenched from my shoulder, baring my upper arm. He stared at it, and so did the giant, breathing his great breaths. "There ain't no mark," he said.

I pulled my shirt across, baring my other arm. There, in the little hollow below my shoulder, was a patch of hard skin, a mark in the shape of a diamond. I had been born with it, though how Weedle could know that was a mystery. It was exactly where he had thought to find it, but on my other arm instead.

"Poz!" shouted Benjamin Penny. "I knew it was you, Smashy."

"It is," said Boggis, suddenly pale. "Living or dead, it's him."

The giant moved away. I could see that I had nothing more to fear from him, nothing to fear from anyone. As though my change were now complete, I had become that mysterious boy I'd lifted from his grave. Inside and out, I was the same—or a mirror image—and everyone believed that I was him in the flesh. Even Midgely believed it, as his only other choice was the impossible notion that I was really a captain's son. Why, I nearly believed it myself.

That afternoon the ship prepared to sail. The hatch was locked down and covered with a heavy grate, and the sailors ran to sailors' chores. Midgely lay against me. There was a smile on his young face, until Penny came to join us.

It didn't seem that Benjamin Penny would be content to be anywhere except right between Midgely and me. He kicked at Midgely's legs to shift them from his way. "Move!" he said.

"No," said Midgely, kicking back. "Does your mother know you're out?"

Many times I'd heard boys taunt each other with that silly question. There was only one answer, and I was surprised to hear Penny trot it out. "Yes, she do," he said in the proper, saucy tone. "But I didn't know the organ man had lost his monkey."

I couldn't help laughing. Benjamin Penny had such an ugly face, on such an awful body, that it was easy to think he had neither heart nor soul inside. But to hear that funny chant come from his lips made me see him now as just a sad boy abandoned by all.

"Sit here," I said, patting the deck on my other side.

I could never please one without upsetting the other. As soon as Penny sat, Midge tugged at my clothes. "Tom," he whispered. "Tom, we don't want him here."

"Oh, let him sit where he likes," I snapped. "You can't see him anyway."

What a terrible thing to say. Instantly I regretted it. Penny laughed, and Midge turned his back, and I—feeling rotten—listened to the strange sounds from above us. Wood and rope worked together, and one man shouted as others sang.

"Smash? What are they doing?" asked Penny.

"Who knows?" I said.

Midgely sighed. "They're setting topsails, you stupids. The helmsman's got her hard over, and she's falling off on the current; it ain't no quiz. They're fitting the capstan bars and—there!—you see? They're weighing anchor."

I heard the sailors singing, and the anchor winding in. I felt the ship slide forward. From the front came a thud.

"Anchor's up," said Midge. "They're hoisting the fore-sails now. They're setting the main course, see."

Through the grating in the hatch I saw a white sail billow open. It flapped and curled around the edge, then tightened in a swooping curve. Water gurgled against the wood behind me. In a rattle of canvas the huge square sail swung across the grate.

"They've come about," said Midge. "Wind's behind them now. They're running for the river."

He said all this with his dead eyes open, seeing nothing. But through his blindness I could look beyond the shadows where we lay. Not everything I understood, yet everything I saw. Our ship added sail upon sail. It quickened on its way, flying down the river, a brown hull under towers of canvas. It flitted past shouting bargemen, heeling to the left as the river burbled down the planks. My heart beat faster; my breaths came deeply. Through the squares of the metal grate I watched shreds of clouds and a silvery bird go streaming by.

The ship hurtled out of the Medway and into the wider Thames. The sails cracked and tightened; the wind made a whistle through the ropes. Then the ship rocked forward, and in a moment rocked back, and it lazily rolled to each side. And that was it for me. Old Neptune had me in his arms already, and he squeezed them round my guts. He rattled me and throttled me, and not an hour into our voyage he had me pinned against the deck.

I wasn't the only one with the seasickness, but none suffered so greatly, and none shared the fear that was building inside me.

As the wretched ship galloped out to sea, Midgely soothed me, but Penny only laughed at my slithering, boneless body. "You're turning green," he said.

"Go away," I told him.

"Green as sewer slime."

"Ohh," I groaned. "Leave me alone."

He did, finally, as soon as old Neptune squeezed my breakfast right out of me. Midgely, by then, had gathered a bucket, and he held it for me as he cradled my head in his lap. "It ain't nothing, Tom," he said. "Think of Nelson. Think of trees, Tom, and beaches. Tom, think of our islands."

I did that—both of us did—as our ship battered its way to the Foreland. We sat on our favorite sunny beaches, with coconut trees above us. We heard the parrots chatter, and the natives drumming at their village. Then came a clamor of canvas and wood, of voices shouting and feet at a run.

"We're coming about," said Midge. "We're heading for the Channel, Tom."

The ship settled onto a new course. It leaned harder to the side, and hurled itself from wave to wave. Creaking like a bag of cats, the hull trembled from end to end. "That's the masts working," said Midge. "They shake the whole ship."

Waves bashed against the bow, each boom of the sea sending a shudder through the timbers. Gallons of water came thundering onto the deck, splattering against the iron grate in bursts of greenish white, raining coldly on our bodies. Soon a sailor appeared there, and another, and they tore the grating open.

I thought we were about to sink. I tried to get up, but the deck was too slippery, my legs too weak. "Save yourself, Midgely!" I shouted.

He only smiled. "Ain't nothing, Tom," he said. "Why, this ain't nothing at all."

As always, he was right. The sailors had only opened the hatch to give us food and water. Down came bloated skins and sacks, falling as though at a slant to land at the side of the ship. Then came the blankets, some thudding down in tight rolls, some fluttering like wounded birds. Midgely collected his share and more, but I wanted neither food nor drink.

The grating was closed again. Over the top, sailors stretched tarpaulins that the sunlight turned to sheets of gold. In a moment they were soaked with spray, and their glistening wetness gave our space a pleasant, shadowed glow. I was glad that the sails and the rushing clouds were hidden at last.

"That's better," I said. "I like the darkness, Midge."

"Oh," he said. "It ain't night already, is it? What a ripping day we've had."

That was the first I knew that his eyes were getting worse. He hadn't seen the tarpaulins, nor even sensed the difference in the light. I looked into his eyes and saw them grayer than before. He yawned, then stretched out at my side, nearly covered in blankets.

"Tom?" he asked. "Where's that horrible boy? He ain't near, is he?"

"No," I said.

"You'll keep him away, won't you? If he comes back, you'll chase him off?"

"Oh, Midge," I said. "Does it really matter?"

"Yes," he said, whispering now. "It does."

"Why?"

"I shouldn't even tell you, Tom," he said. "I should turn the other cheek." He sighed. "But he's the one, Tom. That Benjamin Penny, he's the one that blinded me."

I wanted to get up right then and give Penny the thrashing I'd given to Weedle. But I wanted as well to lie right where I was and never move again. I managed only to lift my head and stare across the ship. Weedle had his face in a bucket, and Boggis was rocking and moaning. Between them, Benjamin Penny sat laughing.

"Please don't smash him, Tom," said Midgely. "Promise you won't."

"But, Midge," I said.

"No!" He pinched my sleeve in his fingers. "Say you won't do nothing. Promish you'll be a meek."

I gave him my word. Then Midgely eased me down again, and I fell at last into a woozy sleep.

Because of Midgely, the struggles and battles had ended. It was an uneasy peace belowdecks as we sailed to the south, but a peace nonetheless. Weedle and his lot kept to one side of the ship, Midgely and I to the other. Benjamin Penny seemed caught in the middle, until my coldness finally drove him off. Then he made a place at the giant's side, and his horrid laughter often rang through the ship. But from the glances he gave me, and the dark looks he fixed on Midge, I knew he housed a bitterness and jealousy. He could never forgive nor forget.

twenty-three

FACE TO FACE WITH KING NEPTUNE

Six weeks into our journey, I still hadn't seen our mad captain. Carrots said he left his cabin only at night, to pace the deck from dark to dawn and mutter at the moon.

But the ship I knew well. I had applied myself to it as I had once sweated over Greek and arithmetic, and through Midgely's teachings I'd learned why the sails were trimmed to be flat one hour and full the next. I'd learned their names, and the names of the ropes that worked them—the sheets and braces and whatnot—and saw the sense in all the many tangles. I'd even begun to see why my father loved his world of oceans.

I looked forward now to my turns on deck. I dared to look beyond the rail at the patterns of the waves and the puffy clouds always in the distance. I sat high on the stack of lumber below the foremast, a place where the sailors liked to lounge in the sun on the old tarpaulin covers, where the fiddler sometimes played. On our forty-second day I crept to the front of the ship. I clung to the rigging that braced the bowsprit and stared straight down at the ship's very bow slicing through the water, shredding it open in glistening curls.

"She's making miles," I said to Midge, and felt very much the sailor.

He and I were never apart. We spent as much time as ever in his world of islands, but began to explore a new one as well. Convinced that I was the Smasher, he begged to hear stories about my gang of urchins, and I amused myself by spinning the wildest tales I could imagine. I told of dark deeds in dark alleys, casting myself as a Robin Hood who helped the lame and the blind, preying only on Mr. Goodfellow, who appeared in every tale—under a different name—and suffered more agonies than all the poor old Greeks rolled together.

Midge didn't really believe the stories, but pretended he did. And over time I told him all, even of my diamond. The old blind mud lark became a rich man with a fancy walking stick, but that was the only thing I changed. Midgely listened, then followed my tale with another, about an old king and a pirate named Captain Jolly.

It was a story more strange than any of mine, more tangled than a mystery. It was about a jewel called the Jolly Stone, a fabulous diamond that brought ruin to all. It started on a ship, with a battle in the moonlight, and moved a hundred places through a hundred years. And it ended below the Tower of London, with a woman on a white horse galloping to her death. "In her hand was the cursed stone," said Midge. His voice slurred. "No one sheen it ever shinsh."

The story gave me chills. If there was any truth in it at all, if my diamond was really the Jolly Stone, I had found the biggest one in all creation. And with it, a plague of misery and pain.

"Didn't it make *anyone* happy?" I asked.

"Oh, all of them," said Midge. "But not for long. If I was you, I'd leave it where it is. Even if it ain't that Jolly Shtone."

"But think of the riches," I said. "I could have my own carriage, and so could you. We could both be gentlemen, Midge."

"Me?" He laughed. "Me, a gentleman? Holy jumping mother of Moses, Tom, I ain't no gent. I don't want no part of that."

He never asked where my diamond was. He never spoke of it again. For Midge, the only thing that mattered was the ship. It carried us along in gales and calms, in cold and searing heat. The Goodfellow flag flew always above us, and the farther south we went, the hotter the days became, and the more fitful was the wind. For hour upon hour—sometimes for a full day or more—the ship didn't move forward at all. But it rocked to and fro in an agonizing fashion. Far to the right, then far to the left, the masts swung like pendulums. The sails flapped, the yards creaked, the blocks and slack lines slammed on the canvas. And my sickness returned.

Midge said we were in the doldrums. It was the perfect name for a place with no wind and no shelter from the sun. It was so hot that the pitch melted on the deck, and globs of black—hot as coals—fell upon us like a hellish rain. The scorching sun seemed to climb through the rigging, up the shrouds as noon approached, every day a little higher. From the angles and the heights, I calculated that the sun would balance on the topgallant yard one day. And when it did, we would cross the equator.

"Oooh, we'll see Neptune then," said Midgely.

"Go on," I said. I thought he was pulling my leg.

"It's true. King Neptune and his court, they board every ship when it crosses the line."

"Why?"

"Why not?" said Midge. "It's his sea, ain't it? The whole ship turns out to meet him, Tom."

It took a week to prove him right. Then the sun mounted the topgallant yard, and not an hour later we were taken up on deck. The sails were set at odd angles, the ship turned into the wind, skidding sideways up big, rounded waves. "She's hove to," said Midgely. "We must be waiting for Neptune."

There were three tubs of water set against the rise to the afterdeck. Planks and barrel hoops lay beside them, and all the sailors had gathered. Sunburned and laughing, they sprawled on the stack of lumber and perched along the rail. Suddenly they cheered, and up from the sea came Neptune with his trident in his hand. His hair was green, his face a terrible red, and he rose from the ocean in a water tub.

It took me only a moment to see that Neptune was really the old blacksmith, wrapped in a strange cloak. His hair and beard were seaweed, clotted by oatmeal and tar, and his face was painted with ochre. Three of his Tritons were jammed with him in the tub, all bellowing as the sailors brought it inboard and tipped out the king of the sea.

He tumbled onto the deck in a most unkingly way. Then up he leapt and roared, "Who goes here? Bring me the captain, I say."

His Tritons went running, leaping to the barrels, up to the afterdeck. The sailors parted, and a man appeared.

It wasn't the madman Carrots had spoken of. He had no bloodstained lash, no evil in his eyes. I looked at him and gasped, for I knew him very well.

Our captain was my father.

He came with his familiar smile, in his familiar walk,

and my heart glowed to see him. He looked younger than I remembered, his face burned by the sun, his eyes shining. He looked down at King Neptune. "We're bound for New South Wales," he said.

Neptune stroked his beard. "Have any among you never crossed the line?"

What followed was an hour of utter delight. The planks were set atop the barrels, and three by three the boys went forward to meet the court of Neptune. They paid tribute to him with little songs and silly dances, and Neptune granted freedom to some, but not very many. The rest were sat up on the planks, and the royal barbers came forward to shave them. With enormous scrubbing brushes, the barbers applied a foul lather of grease and tar, then took up the iron hoops for razors. At the last touch of the blade the planks were pulled away, and down went the boys into the barrels. Some squawked and shouted, but others laughed, and none more than Benjamin Penny. His webbed hands splashing, he frolicked in the water like one of the dolphins that often played round the ship.

It was hard to wait for my turn, as I longed to cry out to my father, to run and put my arms around him. I imagined the look of surprise and delight that would come to his face when he saw me. But when I stepped forward he turned to a sailor's chore and didn't see me dance my little jig, nor sit atop the plank. When he looked again, my face and head were coated with lather.

The royal barber scraped at me. Too soon the plank was pulled away. I tumbled breathless into the water.

It was not as deep as I was tall, but the wooden barrel was slick with lather. I struggled and gasped, but the ship roared with laughter. King Neptune, thinking my struggles a game, thrust his trident into the tub, and whenever I rose to the surface he pushed me down again.

In desperation I grabbed the trident and gave it a mighty pull. To my great surprise, I hauled the king of the ocean head over heels into the barrel. His beard floated off; his wig tangled in my arms. I breathed water into my lungs and couldn't cough it out. Down I sank in the warmth and the darkness, until my face touched the bottom of the barrel.

Hands hauled me out. They were my father's hands; I knew them right away. They plucked me from the water and held me above it. There was his face, peering into mine. It was such a shock he got that he dropped me again, and old Neptune himself had to fish me out in a dead faint.

When I woke, the game was over. I was sitting on the deck, my back against the barrel, dribbling rivers of water on the wood. The boys were gone, the gratings replaced. Neptune and his Tritons and barbers had shed their green wigs, and now stood looking foolish in their robes and red-painted faces.

My father was kneeling beside me, patting my hand. "Tom?" he said, when he saw me awake. "Is it really you?"

"Yes, Father," I said.

Tears bubbled from his eyes, shining in the sun. Then his arms wrapped around me, and all of him trembled. "Oh, if I'd only known you were here," he said. "All these weeks you've been so close. But it wasn't in my heart to come on deck when it was full of hungry, wretched lads. I couldn't bear to look at them." He touched my arms, my hair, as though he wasn't sure that I was real. "But here you are."

His dark hair, windblown into tangles, ruffled in front of my eyes. He looked at gawking Neptune, at all the gawking sailors, and he grinned. "Set the topsails, set the jibs," he told them. "Set the staysails, if you please, and steer for Table Bay." Then he helped me to my feet and took me to his cabin.

There, in the stern of the ship, I stretched out flat on his bunk. He gave me raisins and cheese and a glass of small beer. He sent for oranges. For *oranges!*—even the word was delicious. Then we asked each other, with the same wonder, "How did you end up here?"

I went first. I told him how I'd gone into the fog and found a diamond. "Father, it's the most fabulous diamond," I said. "It might be the Jolly Stone and—"

"I don't give a hang about that," he said. "I want to know about *you.*"

So I told him about the blind man and old Worms, about the boy in the grave, my dead twin. "He was exactly like me," I said. "But you know that; you saw him. Mr. Goodfellow took you there."

"He made me bargain first." My father walked to the windows at the stern, opened one, and let in the sound of water and waves. "He wouldn't take me until I agreed to his terms."

"You promised to sail his ships," I said.

My father nodded as he stood staring out the window.

"Will you carry slaves for him?"

"Slaves?" cried my father, turning to face me. "Good God, no, my boy."

"The ship's a slaver," I said.

"Was," said he. "Seized and sold; a bargain for Mr. Goodfellow. Lord knows what he's up to now. He has sent along every chart of the Java Sea, so I'm bound to be sailing home by way of Borneo. I'm to meet his agent in New South Wales, and then I'll see the cut of his jib. I suspect there will be some odd sort of cargo. But slaves?" Father shook his head. "He knows it's forbidden."

"He's not above it," I said. "He's done worse."

186

My father nodded. "Well, Mr. Goodfellow shall get his comeuppance," he said. "That's one cockroach I want to see crushed. We'll land at Table Bay and I'll quit the ship. We'll go home together and—"

"No," I said. "They'll only put you back in prison, and me in irons."

"Then I'll sign you aboard as crew."

"As crew?" I said. "Dad, I'm afraid of the sea."

"No wonder why," he told me, still gazing through the window. I couldn't look at his back without seeing all the water beyond him, the trail of the ship laid in white streaks across the waves. "There are things I never told you, Tom. About the night you were born."

I pressed my hand against my arm, feeling the hardness of my scar. I thought I knew what he was about to say.

"Your mother had a bad time of it, Tom," he told me. "On the night you were born I feared I would lose her." He drew back from the window. "I went to find the doctor, but the wind was so fierce. I had to crawl up the Beacon Hill on hands and knees. I thought the rain would drown me. I fetched the house, but the doctor wasn't there. He had slipped his moorings that morning for Chatham, and there was nothing to do but take your mother to see him."

I pulled my legs up on the bunk. I sat in its little nook as the ship rambled through the waves.

"The wind pushed us down to the wharf like the hand of God. I put your mother in a boat and shipped the oars, and off we went. Row? I couldn't do that. The wind sailed us down the river, and the best I could do was steer with the oars. But one was carried away in a moment. It flew from my hand, Tom." He reached his arm toward the cabin's swinging lamp. "It leapt from the pins and soared up in the wind like a wooden bird, tumbling end over end."

My father poured himself a glass of the small beer and drank it in a gulp.

"In all the seven seas I've never seen a storm like that. The wind was solid spray. It tore your mother's bonnet into shreds. The waves tumbled over us, and the sound—well, you couldn't imagine it, Tom. And that's when you were born, right there in the boat."

He had never told me any of this. But now I knew why I'd always feared the water.

"You were born feetfirst," he said. "I pulled you out and . . ." His fingers touched the window ledge. "Tom, it was terrible. I thought you had two heads. The water ran with blood, and your mother let out such a shriek of pain. Then two heads suddenly appeared, one turned up and one turned down."

"My twin," I said. "We were joined together, weren't we? We were joined at the shoulder."

He settled onto a bench, as though his knees had buckled. "There was a bit of skin; that was all. I took out my knife and cut you apart." His face was pale now. "I couldn't hold the both of you, Tom. God knows I tried, but I couldn't. In the wind, in those seas, with the boat full of water . . ."

He sat quietly, his shoulders hunched. When he spoke again, it was in a whisper. "If I live to be a hundred, I'll never forget it. That little pink baby—my son—tumbling away into the storm. He was kicking, Tom. His feet, they were kicking. And the last thing—he opened his eyes. He looked right at me, and then he was gone."

At last I knew it all. We had been more than brothers, I and my mysterious twin. We had once been one person, sharing our blood and very essence. By what chance had my father saved me and lost my twin? If his hands had clutched the other baby instead of me, would I have lived the Smasher's life?

I saw that I would spend the rest of my days wrestling with those questions, and others. Was the wickedness that was in my brother in me as well? Were we fated all along to be joined again?

I leaned my weight on my father's shoulder. I felt his heart beating in his chest. "What about Mother? Is she . . ." I couldn't say it. The heartbeats suddenly quickened. "Does she still breathe?"

"Yes," he said. "But barely. She scarcely knows who she is."

"Then I won't ever see her again," I said. "I'll be gone seven years."

"No, you won't," he said. "I'd sooner leave you in hell than in New South Wales."

His heartbeats came so loud and fast that I turned my head away, not wanting to hear their desperate drumming. "What else can you do?" I said.

"We'll think of something, Tom." My father put his hand on the back of my neck and pressed his fingers there. It was an old, familiar gesture, but I realized it had been many years since he'd made it. "I'm an old sailor, and you're a dab hand with the planning, so together we can do it. But we'll do our thinking here in my cabin."

"No, I have to go back below," I said. "I've got a friend there who needs me. He's half blind and—"

"We'll bring him up!" cried Father. "The two of you can—"

"But we'd be noseys then," I said. "We can't be noseys."

"Of course not," said Father, with a smile that warmed my heart. "You're a fine lad, Tom. But I don't think I have it in my heart to send you below."

"I don't mind," I said. "I'm important now."

"Are you?" he said, still smiling. "Because of your diamond?"

"No. Because my father's Redman Tin."

It was still strange to see my father blush. He was embarrassed, but pleased. "Well, never mind that," he said. "We've got thinking to do."

The ship heeled in a gust of wind. I heard a creak of wood and a slap of canvas, and felt that funny lurch of the masts at work. Everything Midge had taught me came together, and I *saw* the masts and sails as though the deck weren't there. The wind was rising, the ship hard pressed.

"Father," I said, "I think it's time to reef the topgallant."

author's note

First of all, there was never a hulk called the *Lachesis*. Had Tom Tin been a real boy, he would have gone to a ship called *Euryalus*.

She was a frigate, a fifth-rater of thirty-six guns. She served as a warship for twenty-two years, and fought at Trafalgar, where the British navy clashed with the fleets of the French and the Spanish. She was the eyes of Lord Nelson, shadowing the enemy fleet and signaling its actions. When the battle was over, she bore the news of the great victory, and the death of Nelson, home to England.

In 1825, *Euryalus* was stripped of her masts and her guns, of all that had made her a warship, and her bare hulk was chained to the riverbed not far from the Chatham dockyard. She became a prison for boys. For eighteen years the hulk sat there, settling into its own waste and filth as the boys came and went on their way to Australia.

But in all that time, it seems, no one recorded even the most basic details of the ship. Today, historians can't agree whether rows of barred cells divided the decks, or whether the boys were sorted into any divisions of age or character. They don't know where the workroom was, or what the chapel was like, or just where the boys ate and slept. The only thing that's certain is that the real *Euryalus* was more terrible than my *Lachesis*.

It's hard to imagine how crowded life was on the hulk. Though the number of boys varied greatly, at the time of Tom Tin there were nearly four hundred housed in a hull about the same length and width of two tennis courts laid end to end. Take a pair of ships the size of *Euryalus,* chop off their bowsprits, and you could sit them side by side in an Olympic-size swimming pool.

Sickness spread quickly among boys not properly fed. The strong ones preyed on the weak, and the weak simply withered away.

There was a hospital to care for them—a ship called *Canada,* or a facility on shore—but it was dreadfully hard for the boys to get there. At a time when there were three hundred convicts on *Euryalus,* there were only seven in the hospital. Yet the boys deliberately broke their arms, or scalded their skin and encouraged infection, or tumbled themselves down the ladders, just for a chance to get there. Among them was a boy of six and a half, whose story was told to a government inquiry by Thomas Dexter, a longtime convict and, at the time, a nurse at the Chatham hospital.

"I believe he was sentenced at Birmingham, from the Warwick assizes, and the judge asked his mother would she take him home again provided a lenient sentence was passed, and she refused to do it," said Dexter. "He was consequently sentenced to transportation, that he might be taken care of."

Dexter met the boy in the hospital. "He died very shortly after he came in," he said.

This wasn't unusual. According to Dexter, many boys died in the hospital. "I have had patients . . . who have declared they have not tasted meat for three weeks together," he said, "but they have been obliged to give their portions to those nobs, and they have been feeding themselves upon gruel and the parings of potatoes."

He had nothing but contempt for a system that sent boys to the hulks.

"Frequently when I have seen it in a newspaper that a judge has sentenced a boy out of mercy to the hulks," he said, "I have made the observation that was it a child of mine I would rather see him dead at my feet than see him sent to that place."

For the boys, the best hope was to be transported. Very few were pardoned, and though many tried to escape, even fewer did that. Apart from serving out his sentence, a boy's only release from the ship was transportation.

Tom Tin is sentenced to seven years' transportation for killing a man. Oten Acres receives the same sentence for stealing a sheep, but this isn't out of line. Sentences of transportation were set at seven years, at fourteen years, or for life. Boys under thirteen—and later fifteen—were rarely transported. The youngest ones, like Midgely, were kept on the hulk until they reached that age. On *Euryalus* were boys as young as five, who would not reach the age for transportation before their sentences were finished. But the rules were loose, and boys were sometimes sent beyond the seas at the age of nine.

Britain began transporting her convicts in the seventeenth

century. Many went to America, until the War of Independence brought an end to that. Others went to Canada. But it was the settlement of Australia that opened a floodgate for transports. In the famous First Fleet of 1787, almost eight hundred convicts were sent from England to New South Wales. Others followed every year afterward, until transportation ended in 1857.

Samuel Ogilby was a boy convict in 1835. He was ten years old, sentenced to seven years' transportation for the theft of a jacket and a waistcoat. He told the government inquiry that he was hoping to be transported, though he had little idea of what awaited him in Botany Bay. "I might like it or I might not," he said. "I have heard that they used to work in chains, but that those who had good characters were sold to masters." He didn't mind which it would be; he wanted only to leave the hulk. "I do not like this place," he said.

I was disappointed that I couldn't put Tom Tin on that real ship. But to suggest that I knew what it must have been like to be on it seemed an injustice both to the hulk and to the boys who passed through it.

More than the name is different. I combined three hulks into one, hoping to find at least a fair representation of conditions for the convict boys. From *Euryalus* come the details of Tom Tin's numbing routine, his silent work and silent meals and silent trudging round the deck. His nobs and noseys, his sea of hammocks and fears of the locked-down ship, are also drawn from accounts of *Euryalus.*

Some of the other details of the boys' lives come from the hulk *Bellerophon.* In her day, she had been another famous fighting ship. Launched in 1786, she was a ship of the line, a seventy-four. Known fondly by her crew as the *Billy Ruffian,* she fought at the Glorious First of June and at the Nile and Trafalgar, and carried Napoleon from France after his surrender in 1815. But the following year, *Bellerophon* was hulked, and sat at Sheerness for nearly a decade. From 1824 to 1825, her great hull was the first prison ship to be set aside solely for boys. Before then, boys and men had been lumped together, and there were boys scattered through all of the hulks.

Bellerophon was much larger than *Euryalus*. The boys lived in big, barred cells. From dark to dawn, guards patrolled the corridors between them. It might have been a better place, but *Bellerophon* lacked something special for the boys—a workroom. When one was built into *Euryalus,* the boys moved to a new home.

Tom Tin's lavish chapel comes from the hulk *Defence*. It's shown clearly in one of the few etchings that illustrate real life aboard the hulks. Higher than two decks, lit by skylight and chandelier, it was large enough to seat every convict and officer. The altar was enormous, but there was no crucified figure atop it.

The kindly chaplain in this story is based very loosely on the first chaplain of *Euryalus*. Horrified by the conditions on the hulk, he did everything he could to better things for the boys. All he accomplished was to have himself moved swiftly to another hulk. His place was taken by a man who measured success by the silence of the boys at chapel, and by the number who learned by heart long passages from the Bible.

When I've told parts of this story to people, I've sometimes been asked, "What about girls? What happened to them?"

Only men and boys were sent to the hulks. Girls who strayed into crime fared better. For them were reformatory schools, and instruction in reading and writing, ciphering, and needlework. The girls were kept hard at work, doing laundry and all the industrial chores of a household. After their time in reformatory, it was hoped, girls would be capable of finding positions in any sort of domestic work.

The boys had no training. One witness at the 1835 inquiry said it wasn't fair to send untrained boys to Australia. But it wasn't the boys he worried about; it was Australia.

"To transport them immediately," he said, "without having previously trained them to labor and endeavored to instil into them habits of industry, is to burthen a colony with a worthless and a useless set of vagabonds."

acknowledgments

I would like to thank the following people for their help with this story and the historical information within it. They led me through a huge range of puzzling subjects, from nineteenth-century crime and the English prison system to naval architecture and the speed of three-legged horses.

Kathleen Larkin, research librarian at the Prince Rupert Public Library in Prince Rupert, British Columbia, Canada.

Dr. Heather Shore, lecturer in social and cultural history at the University of Portsmouth, England, and author of *Artful Dodgers,* a study of youth and crime in nineteenth-century London.

Professor David Taylor, dean of the School of Music and Humanities at the University of Huddersfield, England, and author of *Crime, Policing and Punishment in England.*

Jeremy Mitchell, curator of historic photographs and ship plans at the National Maritime Museum in London, England.

J. Kevin Ash, coroner in Prince Rupert, BC, Canada, and world traveler.

Allison Wareham, librarian at the Royal Naval Museum at HM Naval Base (PP66), Portsmouth, England.

Robert Gardiner, British naval historian at Chatham Publishing in London, England, and author of numerous books on historic ships.

Miss E. M. Worby of HM Prison Service Museum in Rugby, England.

Stephen Nye, assistant curator of Guildhall Museum in Rochester, England.

Jean Lear of the Archives and Local Studies Centre in Strood, Rochester, England.

The staff of the Humanities Enquiries Service at the British Library in London, England.

Sarah Perry of the Bradbourne Carriage Driving Club in London, England.

Lucy McCann, archivist at the Bodleian Library of Commonwealth and African Studies, at Rhodes House, Oxford, England.

Alison Marsh, curator of the Historic Dockyard at Chatham, England.

Michael Carter from the Centre for Kentish Studies in Maidstone, England.

Dr. Peter Reid from Robert Gordon University in Aberdeen, Scotland.

Peter Davis of Zeist, the Netherlands.

Andrea Ryce of the BC Children's Hospital Family Resource Library in Vancouver, Canada.

Pat Murray, Matt Cooper, and Nigel Tkachuk of the Prince Rupert Public Library, Prince Rupert, Canada.

Cheryl Morrison and Tim MacDonald of Northwest Community College in Prince Rupert, Canada.

Raymond Lawrence of Nanaimo, Canada, a storehouse of knowledge, and my dad.

about the author

Iain Lawrence studied journalism in Vancouver, British Columbia, and worked for small newspapers in the northern part of the province. He settled on the coast, living first in the port city of Prince Rupert and now on the Gulf Islands. An avid sailor, he wrote two nonfiction books about his travels along the coast before turning to children's novels. With *The Convicts,* Lawrence returns to his favorite place and period—nineteenth-century England. He remembers being on a family outing in southern Ontario when he saw a prisoner being transported to the federal penitentiary in Kingston. Though he was only six or seven years old, he never forgot the sight of the man peering from the barred window in the back of the armored truck. "There we were, all playing in the grass at a roadside rest stop," says Lawrence, "and there he went, shrinking down the highway on a bright summer day. For a moment I looked at him, and he looked at me, and it was enough to give me an everlasting horror of prisons." The only time Lawrence spent in prison was when he was locked in the jail cell of a police station during a school tour in fourth grade.

Iain Lawrence is the author of six other acclaimed novels. His novels for younger readers include the High Seas Trilogy: *The Wreckers, The Smugglers,* and *The Buccaneers;* as well as *Lord of the Nutcracker Men.* His novels for young adults are *Ghost Boy* and *The Lightkeeper's Daughter.*

You can find out more about Iain Lawrence at www. iainlawrence.com.